JESSICA

*EVERYONE HAS A
SECRET*

D. N. WATTS

JESSICA: EVERYONE HASA SECRET

Second Edition, June, 2021.

Copyright © 2021 Debby-Ann Watts

Written by D. N. Watts

Contact Info: ephiphany.debby@gmail.com

*For anyone who needs
a second chance at love*

1

After her conversation with her Doctor, Jessica drove directly to the beach. She parked opposite the boardwalk, shut her engine off and lowered her window, allowing the hot afternoon air inside. She pushed her back against the seat of the car as realization set in. She was pregnant and the scary part was, she didn't know who her baby's father was.

A flood of tears came suddenly and with such force that she could hardly breathe. Her soul felt ill. She was possibly carrying a child for a man other than her husband's. For a brief moment, she considered not telling anyone that the baby might be Ron's, outside of Trey and Charmaine, no one else knew she'd slept with her ex, maybe she could convince Trey that she was pregnant with his baby. That would be a secret worth taking to her grave.

She thought that she could have the baby and her

and Trey would live happily ever after. Sadly her life was no fairytale. Jessica spent the next two hours going over her options and by 5:00 p.m., she was still clueless as to what to do. She still had a few months before she actually started showing. But, she had to think of a way to tell Trey that, not only was she pregnant but that Ron might be the baby's father before too late. She grabbed a tissue from the cubby hole and dabbed at her wet eyes. Using the crumpled tissue in her hand she wiped the sweat forming on her brows while she pondered how she found herself in her current mess. She was sweating like a pig, not from the heat of the humid day, it was from her increasing anxiety and stress.

Outside of the obvious, she was not sure how she felt about being pregnant just three months shy of getting married, she was not ready to be a mother, it didn't matter who the father was. She had prayed that the Plan B worked after sleeping with Ron and now she wasn't sure it did. For her, it would be better to be pregnant for her husband than her ex. There was only one option, she needed to have an abortion before she got further along in her pregnancy. She decided to schedule the appointment the very next day. A fresh flood of tears washed over her face as she faced a decision she never thought she would have in a million years.

She felt completely alone and confused. She desperately wanted to talk to Charmaine, she needed confirmation that what she was about to do, was somewhat understandable under the circumstances. Her marriage would not survive this blow; she knew that Trey would leave her for good, that's something she couldn't handle again. Damn, she wouldn't even get to enjoy her honeymoon, which would have to be pushed back once more, she would need time to heal from her procedure, she didn't know what to expect after, she'd never had one before, but from what she heard from friends, the recovery can be messy and bloody.

She cleaned her face with a wet wipe and rested her head in her hands. The sun was searing through her front screen so she flipped the visor down to block the bright rays from her damp eyes. The beach looked so inviting, she wished she had a swimsuit to take a nice dip and enjoy the warm salty water. Anyway, she wasn't there to swim. Groping around in her bag she found a half filled bottle of water, she took huge gulps and returned it to her bag. Her memories drifted to Ron, she was once so eager to marry him and have his kids, sigh! How quickly love can turn to hate and oh boy did she hate him. There was definitely a thin line between love and hate.

She hated herself even more for being in his home

alone, she remembered feeling uneasy before stepping foot inside of his condo but she shrugged it off, if only she had listened to her instincts, she would not be considering an abortion at this very moment. She wanted nothing to do with Ron and she certainly didn't want to have his baby. She took a deep breath. She had made her decision. At 6:00 p.m., she started her engine and headed home. She'd stayed at the beach longer than anticipated and Trey would be home or on his way home.

Jessica pulled up to her curb and parked. She gathered herself and exited her car. Trey came up behind her with a barking Max from a walk around the block. She fluffed Max's mane and they all walked inside. Trey grabbed a bottled water from the refridgerator and drank the entire thing in one swig. Jessica was trying to act normal but she was failing miserably. He removed Max's leash, freeing him to roam as he wished.

He sat next to her at the kitchen island.

"Are you ok?" he asked suspiciously.

She nodded yes. She felt emotionally shaken.

"Oh, before I forget, your doctor called. She wants you to pick up a prescription for your prenatal vitamins, she forgot to give you the prescription." Trey watched her reaction closely.

Jessica was sure she'd collapsed on the floor, her

body felt heavy and rigid. She bitterly wished she had the ability to disappear. Barely moving her shoulders she stretched her right hand down and using her fingertips, she felt around the hard plastic of the bar chair beneath her, thankfully, she was still seated at the island and not passed out on the floor.

"Are you pregnant?" His glare felt like heated coals melting through her body. Her own saliva turned dry and was choking her at the back of her throat, she was sure dust would have puffed out of her mouth whenever she spoke.

"Jessica?" He called again.

Fucking shit. Fuck. Fuck. Fuck.

"Yes. I saw my Doctor today." She still had not made eye contact with him.

"Why didn't you call me and tell me?"

"It was a shock to me, I guess I forgot."

"Hmmm." Trey was no idiot, he knew something was up, neither did he forget that she slept with her ex a few months back.

"How far along are you?"

"I'm not sure yet." Her throat was so dry, her voice sounded croaky. She drained the few remaining droplets of water left in his bottle.

"Hmmm."

"I hate when you say that! Got damn, it's fricking annoying?" she snapped.

5

Trey ignored her outburst. "Is it his?" His gut wrenched and contracted as he waited for her answer.

"I don't know." She looked at him as though seeing him for the very first time. His face carried no expression but she could feel the tension building around them. A thick vein popped up in the centre of his forehead. He turned and slid out of his seat. He grabbed a cold beer from the refridgerator before kicking open the patio door. The pain and hurt hit him hard, he gulped his beer trying to fight back his own tears.

Jessica was helpless to help him in his torment, she too was stressed and she also needed comforting, she regrettably recognized that she was to blame for his upset. She pushed herself from the chair and sat next to him on the patio. She wrapped her arms around him as he sobbed uncontrollably. She wanted to tell him how sorry she was, she had said it to him so many times, she doubt it would have any effect on him.

"This is all your fault," he hissed. She was shocked and crushed by his words.

"Trey, please..."

"I'm not raising another man's baby." He was seething. "And I'm not staying in a marriage with someone who'd easily fuck her ex and stupidly get pregnant." He was practically foaming at the mouth.

Jessica felt she deserved his hate, after all she was

the one who cheated. She straightened her back as her heart was pounded by the venomous words he hurled at her, his rage and fury spilling out of him; he'd never really told her how he felt about her sleeping with Ron. When he returned home from the hotel, they never discussed how he felt emotionally; in retrospect she guessed they had swept his feelings under the rug. When Trey was finally finished ripping her a new asshole, he was very quiet.

Jessica was shocked, humiliated and embarrassed. She knew that Trey loved her and she also knew her betrayal damaged a part of him. Without saying a word, she stood and went directly to her bedroom. She filled her tub to the brim, tossing in a few herbs while the hot water flowed in. She locked the bathroom door and undressed, tossing her worn clothes on the floor, she flipped her music on and perched her phone on the top shelf in the bathroom.

She eased her body into the hot water and it relaxed her immediately. Silent tears trickled down her face, Trey had never spoken to her like that before, not even in a serious argument. A choked sob echoed around her, she rolled her shoulders and flexed her neck as she tried removing the achy tension from her head and calming herself. She subconsciously rubbed her stomach.

"What am I am going to do with you now?" she

smiled sheepishly.

Trey finished the last of his beer and grabbed another from the refridgerator. He returned to the patio. He was reeling from a massive headache. He was beyond pissed at Jessica. He honestly did not mean to berate her but he was sick of hearing of Ron's bitch ass. After having him taken care of by a few of his boys he was certain he was well behind them. But, she could potentially be carrying his seed. His head began throbbing painfully, he slumped onto the cold patio floor grunting against the searing pain in his head.

2

Jessica remained in the tub until the water had turned ice cold, however, she didn't notice the icy prickles on her skin. She heard movement beyond the bathroom door. Trey was in the bedroom, she was not ready to face him and her aching heart was recovering from the wounds inflicted by his verbal whipping. She closed her eyes against the frenzied thoughts roaming her mind. She had to end this pregnancy. She had no other choice and she could tell no one. Thirty minutes later, she was bone cold. Stepping out of the water she noticed her skin was wrinkled and creased. She'd sat in the water way too long. She toweled off and slung her robe on, wrapping it loosely around her waist. She brushed her teeth and went into her bedroom.

Trey was resting on the bed, his eyes closed. She dressed silently, choosing a pink fluffy t-shirt and long black sweats. She dropped her robe over her vanity chair and went to the living room. She took the tv remote and started flipping through the channels, she settled on a popular controversial talk show. She was startled when Trey sat next to her.

"I'm sorry." He greatly regretted the way he handled her earlier. "I didn't mean to explode the way I did.

"I'm sorry too," she breathed.

"What are we going to do?"

"I'll handle it."

"How? You know what, don't answer," he said.

"How do you feel?"

"I'm not sure, I know we need to get a DNA test as soon as possible."

Jessica had no intention of being pregnant much longer to need a DNA test. She sat silent, turmoil and dread coursing through her veins. She couldn't even look at him directly. She was uncomfortable and her skin felt cold.

"Will you keep it if it's his?"

She didn't answer. He was aware of her puffy under eye bags and sad demeanor. He backed off and changed the subject.

"Are you hungry?"

"No."

"Ok."

"I'm going to bed," she stomped away from the couch.

She slid slowly beneath her covers exhausted. Her body was tired but her brain was active and alert. She laid on her back, closed her eyes and started counting sheep as she tried to force herself to sleep, at sheep 100 her eyes flew open, she still couldn't fall asleep. She flipped to her side and tried again. Within fifteen minutes she was out. She slept until the next morning.

"You tossed all night long." Trey informed her.

"Yesterday was a lot, it took me awhile before I drifted off to sleep.

Trey was already dressed for work. She sat up, stretched and then tossed the covers off, she didn't want to be late for work. She rushed into the shower, bathed quickly and dressed into casual pants and a matching blouse. She brushed her hair into a low bun and peeled out of the house. She met Trey at the door as he was leaving.

"See you later!" he said shyly.

"Yea. Bye." They would have normally kissed goodbye but that was now out of the question.

Jessica unlocked her car door and adjusted her seat. She peeped at Trey through her rearview mirror. He was flinging architectural drawings onto his backseat. His fury from last night seeped into her mind and she shook the image away and started her engine, as pulled away from the curb and tooted her horn at him. While sitting in traffic, she pulled her phone out and contacted the specialty clinic that dealt with abortions. She gave them a fictitious name and scheduled her appointment for her abortion.

She was miserable at work that entire day, she rescheduled all of her appointments until the next week and moped around her office until the end of the day. At 4:00 p.m., she flung her purse and work bag into her trunk and headed home. When she arrived, Max bounded onto her and she instinctively shielded her stomach from his sudden attack.

"Hey big boy," she sing-songed. He accidently licked her hand as she was about to play in his shiny brown fur. "Ewww Max!" she walked to the kitchen sink and squirted dishwashing liquid in her hands while Max was skirted around her feet; he wanted to play. "You have to wait until daddy gets home, honey." She refilled his bowls with water and treats. Trey soon called her to say he was going to be late.

"Hey dude." Trey smacked and clasped hands with his buddy Cameron when he arrived at the bar. They were seated at the bar of the restaurant not far from Trey's office.

"What's up bro?"

Trey took swig of his beer. "I need some advice man, like some real advice."

"Advice on what?" Cameron ordered a beer and continued..."You and Jess?"

"Yea man, you won't believe what the fuck is happening now."

"What's the problem?" His beastly cold beer arrived and he sampled the delicious brew while watching Trey twitch in his bar seat.

"Jess is pregnant." Trey took another big gulp of his beer. "Basically, she could be pregnant for me or her ex."

"What the fuck!" Cameron was well informed of the issues in Trey's marriage and he was happy that they had rekindled. He knew how close Trey came to asking for a divorce, frankly, he was the one who encouraged him to give Jessica a second chance.

"You have got to be kidding me man."

"Yup. She's only a couple months I guess. I was pissed when she told me and I chewed her ass out bad, and now once again, our entire relationship is in limbo.

I mean I felt bad after but I was mad as fuck."

"Damn man, whatcha' gonna do?"

"That's why I asked you here man, he chuckled, I'm stumped for real."

"I'm stumped too, what's her take on it, does she think the baby could be his?"

"She doesn't know. I think she's gonna have an abortion."

Cameron's eyes stretched wide, "Bro, that could be your baby too?"

"And what if it's not mine, I can't raise another man's baby, especially his."

"Got damn. Yikes. Honestly, I'd take the chance, just on the fact that the baby could be mine. She slept with him one time, you've been together ...."

"It only takes one time," Trey said snidely, "I'd be devastated if she was pregnant for him. I'd have to walk away, as much as I love this woman, I have to love me first."

"I hear you man."

"Can you imagine him coming to our house to collect his kid. I'd fuck his ass up again."

"I'm not going through that shit again with you. I was scared as shit the police was gonna come lock my ass up, my light bright ass wouldn't do good in prison."

"I told you I had you covered," he said heatedly.

"Thought you said she was raped. You can't really

blame her for what's happening now."

"Her ass had no right being alone in his home." Trey could feel his muscles tense as that memory floated before him."

"You need to be clear with her about where you stand if it's his baby. Is she gonna tell him she's pregnant?

"I have no clue, we didn't get that far."

"You need to clear that shit up soon...before she starts showing, you guys need a plan for when Ron comes knocking, cause you know he's gonna put two and two together."

"I'd fuck his ass up if he ever comes near her again," he growled.

"I hope it doesn't come to that." Cameron stressed. "Anyway bro, how's business?"

Trey was happy for the change of topic. "Right now things are looking good, we broke ground on the project in Atlanta, so I'll be in and out of the country as that progresses." They chatted for a little while longer before Cameron had to go. Trey decided to stay at the bar until he felt the effects of the beers sinking in. He paid the bill and set for home.

Trey tossed his keys on the kitchen counter, he was surprised to find Jessica in her office on her laptop. She was hardly ever in there. He tapped lightly on the door and entered, she was seated in front of her desk, staring at her laptop screen. She turned at the sound of his knock.

"I didn't hear you come in?" She smiled up at him and returned her gaze to her screen. She was such a beautiful woman, even during what she termed her 'bad days'.

He drummed his finger on the door frame, before continuing, "We need a plan on how we're going to do about Ron when he finds out you are pregnant."

He took the office chair behind the desk in two swift steps, sitting directly in front of her. "He's not going to make this easy for either of us; I think you know that already."

Her fingers hovered over her keyboard, she was still looking at her screen but her mind was spinning.

She turned to him "Why would we need to do that?" her eyes squinted slightly.

"I don't think you should go through with the abortion," he said evenly.

Her eyes fluttered from the sudden shock of his words. How the hell did he know what she had planned?

"I know you were planning to have an abortion tomorrow. Cancel it," he said firmly.

"Why?" There was no use in denying the truth.

"If you do, then he wins."

"This isn't a game Trey," she lowered her voice

"this *could* be his baby." She didn't think Trey understood how fucked up it was, for her to be pregnant with Ron's baby.

"This baby could also be mine...ours."

Jessica slammed her laptop shut.

To some extent, he was right, but, she was tormented daily with thoughts of Ron pestering her if she didn't have the abortion. He'd probably make their lives a living hell, especially if he suspected Trey had any involvement in his assault.

"But, I don't want to have this baby." She fought back the stinging tears behind her eyes. He was taking away her only way out. She felt guilty from simply saying the words.

"You said you would leave me, if this baby is his, now you want me to have this baby and then what?"

He rubbed his face briskly, "I meant what I said, I can't raise his child."

"Neither can I." Trepidation filled her core from the thought of sharing a baby with an asshole like Ron.

"Until we get a DNA test, you'll tell him it's mine."

"I can simply have the abortion; we can try for *our* baby when we are ready."

"Jessica, you could be killing our own child," he shouted.

"That's a risk we cannot afford to take," she said solemnly. "If this baby is his, then you're leaving me to deal with Ron alone, don't you get that?"

"I won't leave you to deal with him alone, I just wouldn't be your husband anymore."

"Oh my God!" she cried.

"I told you before, I didn't blame you. But we have to deal with the consequences of your actions. If the baby is his, I'll always be there for you Jess, as a friend, that's all I'd be able to offer at that point."

Jessica chuckled ominously. "That's not what you said last night."

"Once the baby is born, we get the test done and then go from there. Please, Jessica, don't have the abortion."

She watched him long and hard.

"Ok. I won't have the abortion."

3

Trey stood and left the room, he sat on the patio, wondering if he had made the right decision. His brows furrowed, it was apparent he had to find another home as soon as possible.

Once he'd gone, she left her office and went to her bedroom, she snatched a pillow from the bed and locked herself in the bathroom, she turned the shower on full blast and perched herself on the side of the tub. After a few deep breaths, she drew the pillow to her face tightly and let loose a blood curdling scream, she relaxed her hands under the pillow, but she didn't remove it from her face. She screamed into the pillow again, strands of her hair stuck to her sweaty face. She rested the pillow on her legs as her heart broke again. Jessica bawled for what seemed like hours, she stopped mid cry when she heard a small knock on the bathroom door.

"Go away," she said in a small voice.

"Jess, unlock the door."

"Trey, leave me alone." Her voice was weak and tired.

The loud rocking of the door handle drew Jessica's attention. She turned the shower off and unlocked the door. She stood in the doorway, glaring at Trey. He stepped towards her and wrapped her lovingly in his arms. His gesture, forced more tears from her eyes, she wailed and mumbled indistinguishable words into his chest and he held her until her body relaxed and her cries abated. He led her to the bed and tucked her under the covers. He looked back at her as he left the bedroom and she was fast asleep.

Trey sat at the kitchen counter, drowning his own tears in several shots of Hennessey. He felt empathy for his wife but that didn't ensure she was pregnant with his seed. The more he thought of his plight, the angrier he became. He flung the empty glass against the wall, shattering it into tiny pieces. The Cognac was hitting him hard, he stumbled to the living room and collapsed on the floor.

Jessica awoke around 2:00 a.m. and Trey was not in

the bed. She shifted onto her back reflecting on her conversation with him. She rested her hand on her stomach, soon she would be showing. She closed her eyes and tried imagining walking around with a huge belly. A small smile spread across her lips. She slid off of the bed, in search of Trey, she found him stretched out on the living room floor with Max sleeping next to him. She went into the kitchen and saw the open bottle of Hennessy and the smashed glass on the floor. She ignored the mess and flipped the house lights off and returned to bed. Her sanity was already at stake.

At 5:00 a.m., she was preparing breakfast for them. Max's barking pierced Trey's eardrums, "Max," he shouted, "quiet down." Max returned to Trey and sat next to him. He clutched his head and sat up, he could hear Jessica in the kitchen. He shuffled to the sink and drank a glass of water.

"How are you feeling?" he asked.

She sighed "What happened in here last night?" she eyed him curiously.

"The same thing that happened to you up there last night," he chuckled.

"Touché."

He hugged her from behind, she stopped pouring the coffee and leaned her head back against his chest.

"We're going to get through this, I promise," he said.

She turned around and kissed him softly on his lips; he took her face in his hands and sucked her lips slowly. She hooked one leg over his thigh, pulling him into her so that she could feel his growing hardness between her opened legs. She sucked air through her teeth when he playfully bit her, sensually nibbling at her neck and trailing kisses to her breasts, his warm tongue swirling around her hardened nipples to her delight. He cupped them in his hands and instantly noticed how much heavier they felt. Soon, they were completely naked grinding against each other.

Trey had forgotten that she was pregnant. He fucked her ruthlessly; her whimpers seemed distant and airy. He returned to her mouth, smashing his lips against hers as he fucked her hard against the kitchen sink. Jessica wrapped her other leg over his other thigh, spreading her legs wider and he plunged into her eagerly. The sudden direct shots into her slippery centre sent Jessica spiraling to a shattering climax, just then Trey's hand accidentally squeezed the spray hose on top of the sink, the icy cold water shot straight into her back. She flew into a frenzy, working her hips wildly against him, her walls tightened around his shaft as her body convulsed viciously. She was sure they were going to rip the got damn counter from the wall. Trey lasted no longer than a minute after her, she was overflowing with cum and he wasn't even close to expelling all of his seed.

Through deep breaths he asked "Will that hurt the baby?" he was concerned.

Jessica was perched precariously at the end of the counter, she slid off careful not to step in the small sperm puddle beneath her. "No, it won't" she managed to say.

Her back was aching from the position she was in on the counter. Her clothes were all over the kitchen, she ripped a few tissues from the roll on the counter and cleaned the puddle from the floor. She picked up their clothes from the floor and walked into her bedroom and stepped into the shower. She asked Trey to pack her a quick breakfast to go while she bathed. It took Jessica twenty minutes to prepare for work, she grabbed the breakfast he had put together for her and stuffed it into her lunch bag. She shouted up the stairs to Trey that she was leaving as he was about to get in the shower to prepare himself for work. She took her usual purse and work bag containing her laptop.

Jessica sat at her office desk, flipping through several messages the Receptionist had passed to her when she entered the building.

"Mr. Bonds, called about 10 times already, he's anxious for a response to his last email to you."

"Tks Syl." Jessica briefly read the note attached to the message and immediately called and canceled her appointment at the specialty clinic and made an appointment with Dr. Crichlow before she called her client.

"Good Morning, Mr. Bonds, this is Jessica. How are you?"

"Yes, Jessica, thank you for returning my call."

"It's no problem, so I received your message from earlier, and I can tell you that the sale should be completed in less than one month.

"This process is becoming increasing ridiculous and frustrating, what's the hold up?"

"The mortgage company was awaiting a report from the structural engineer on the integrity of the building. But, I was assured by the Managing Director, Mr. Sealey that he should have the report in hand by early next week."

"Oh that is wonderful news."

"I'll keep you posted as soon as I receive confirmation from our Attorney."

"Thank you Jessica."

"You are welcome Mr. Bonds. We will chat soon."

Jessica whistled as soon as she ended the call. She was thankful he didn't lose his shit again.

Her office line rang. It was her boss.

"A minute, please."

What the hell did she do now? She walked into his open doorway and closed the door behind her.

He gestured for her to sit.

"I got a call from Ron....he's asked that you no longer have anything to do with the sale of his homes. What's that about Jessica?"

She had to think quick on her feet. "We had gotten into an altercation when I took the agreements over to him to sign, after that, I was done with him."

"Jessica, I don't usually pry into your personal affairs, but, could this altercation have a negative effect on my company?"

"Not at all." She wondered whether to tell him she was pregnant. Not yet, she thought.

"Fine."

"Cool." She returned to her office and shut the door behind her. She walked to her office window, deep in thought. Trey wanted her to continue her pregnancy, to only leave her if the baby wasn't his. What would she do if the baby wasn't his; she would be a single mother. Her parents would be beyond disappointed.

She looked down at her stomach and rubbed her hand in a circular motion over her stomach.

4

She took her breakfast from her lunch bag and filled her hungry belly. She spent the entire day seated at her desk, fielding calls and replying to emails from clients and other agents she co-broke some properties with. Around 4:00 p.m., she started feeling queasy, so she called it a day and made her way home. She unlocked her front door and threw everything on the floor, including her laptop, she took her cell and googled whether she could have a glass of wine while pregnant. From her quick search, she could have at least one glass of wine. She popped open a bottle of red wine and poured herself half of a glass. She took the wine to her couch and switched on the tv.

Her cell rang, as she settled in for some court tv.

"What's going on?" Charmaine asked.

"I'm pregnant?" She said straightforward and with little emotion.

"I'll be right there."

"Uhmm hmm," she tossed the phone next to her. She never took her eyes from the tv.

Charmaine was there within 30 minutes. She was banging on her sister's door like a victim in a horror movie. Jessica opened the door and gazed at Charmaine. She turned and went back to the living room. Charmaine stood timidly above Jessica, observing her sister closely.

"How far along?"

"My appointment is tomorrow."

"What are you gonna do?"

"I wanted to have an abortion today." She was too calm for Charmaine's liking.

"Does Trey know?"

"Yes, he didn't want me to have it done."

Charmaine was petrified to ask the next question. Jessica knew what she wanted to ask.

"I don't know who the father is!" she slowly sipped her wine, eyes still on the tv.

"Shittttt." Charmaine sat next to Jessica on the couch.

"Oh! But that's not the best part," she wagged her finger at Charmaine. "Trey wants me to have the baby but he'll leave me if the baby is Ron's."

"I don't understand that."

"There's still a chance he's the father."

"What are you gonna do?"

"I'm going to have this baby, that's what my husband wants."

"How do you feel about having the baby?"

"I don't want to have any babies right now honestly."

Charmaine rubbed her sister's shoulder, soothingly. "What about Ron?"

"I'll deal with him when the time comes."

Charmaine went to the kitchen and poured herself a glass of wine and returned next to Jessica.

"I can't believe you're having a baby," she smiled awkwardly.

Jessica folded her legs beneath her and stretched her arms between her legs.

"Don't tell anyone yet. I'm not ready to be fake happy."

"I won't. You'll be showing soon, you know that right?"

"Yea, I know."

The sisters sat on the couch making plans for Jessica's interactions with Ron. They were well aware that he would become a serious pain in her ass once he found out she was pregnant. Charmaine poured herself another glass of wine while she waited for Trey to come home, she didn't feel right leaving her sister alone. She could sense that her Jessica was emotional and needed the company. Trey came home two hours later. Charmaine greeted him at the door as she was leaving.

"Hi Char,"

"She told me. How are you?"

"Hanging in, that's all I can do."

They were speaking in hushed tones.

"She's really not in a good place Trey."

"I know."

"Take care of my sister, please. I need you to protect her."

"I will." Trey knew his wife was hurting mentally and emotionally, he knew she did not want to go through with the pregnancy but he needed to be certain of the paternity of the baby. He heard her bawling in the bathroom, the pillow did little to muffle her screams. It hurt him to his core to listen to her screaming repeatedly.

She patted him on his shoulder as she stepped outside.

Trey found Jessica on the couch sitting lotus style enthralled in her tv programme. He kissed her on the cheek.

"Hi baby, how are you feeling?"

"Tired, achy, stressed, pick one?" She snapped.

He pulled her legs out from beneath her and

29

stretched them over his thighs. He took the remote and muted the tv.

"Tell me what I need to do to make this easier for you."

She took a sharp breath.

"I need you to not hate me right now and I need you to not leave me." She was so tired of crying all of the time.

"I don't hate you Jess and I'm not leaving you." He rubbed her thighs gently. He would never tell her that he was actively house hunting. He opened his arms for her to lie in and she crept into his arms; he kissed her forehead and wiped her tear soaked face with his fingers. Jessica's stomach growled loudly.

"Damn, did you eat today?"

"Not since breakfast"

"Ok. I'll whip us up something quick."

He went into the kitchen and raided the fridge; he ended up making their favourite dish, shrimp tacos. When he was finally finished, he plated four for her and six for him. Jessica wolfed down hers in a matter of minutes.

"You were really hungry I see."

Her mouth was too full to answer.

Jessica was thrilled to hear that Trey was willing to stand by her side; it gave her the courage she needed to get through the next seven months.

"I have an appointment with Dr. Crichlow tomorrow."

"Do you want me to go with you?"

"Not necessarily, it's just a routine checkup."

"If you change your mind let me know."

Jessica put her used dish in the sink and told Trey she was going to shower and watch tv in the bedroom. She settled for a cute nightie set and lay across her covers. By the time Trey came to check on her she was snoring lightly.

5

Jessica arrived for her appointment, scared and anxious. She didn't know what to expect. She signed in and waited to be called into the doctor's office. She pulled her cell out and started playing a game she had downloaded for moments like this when she was bored or needed a distraction.

"Jessica!" The nurse called, "the doctor is ready to see you."

She followed the Nurse into another office. She sat just as the doctor walked in.

"Good day Jessica. How are you?"

"I'm fine, thank you."

"So what I am going to do today is examine you and

32

then I'll perform an ultrasound to ensure the viability of the foetus." Doctor Crichlow stepped away from her desk and asked Jessica to lie on the table across the room tucked next to the wall. She'd never seen the computer styled gadget which she assumed was the ultrasound machine.

"Just raise your top for me and lower your skirt a little lower. This liquid is going to be cold."

"Ok," she said, Doctor Crichlow squirted a clear liquid on her stomach and rolled the smooth ball of the handheld device into the liquid, spreading it over her exposed stomach and the top of her pubic area. The doctor pointed to the screen, indicating to Jessica the small dark sac which housed her foetus. Jessica could vaguely make out the tadpole shaped sac.

"Based on the size I'm seeing here, you're about three months pregnant. Congratulations."

"Thank you." The doctor began tapping on the keys of the machine and a loud whirring noise suddenly purred next to the machine. She then wiped Jessica's stomach off and asked her to return to the desk. She handed Jessica a print out of the photos from the ultrasound, a prescription for antenatal vitamins and she also scheduled her for a follow up appointment in one month. Jessica thanked her Doctor Crichlow and exited the room; she walked to the Receptionist and paid for her visit.

Back in her office, she took the photo from her purse and inspected it. She was amazed at the small tadpole that would be her baby. She kissed the photo and placed it back into her purse. Obviously, her hormones were out of whack, one minute she was happy to be pregnant, with Trey's baby of course, the next she was sad, her happiness was always in limbo. Taking a deep breath, she decided to go to the pharmacy during her lunch hour to fill her prescription.

Her office line rang.

"Hey Jessica, are you ready?" It was one of the new interns she was shadowing on her first showing.

"Hi, Pamela, I am. I'll meet you at reception in two minutes."

Jessica snatched her purse and cell and headed out. She reminded Sylvia she would be out with Pamela for a showing; luckily they were travelling in her car. After the showing, she dropped Sylvia off at the office and drove over to the pharmacy in the mall. While she waited, fourth in line, she pulled her phone from her purse and called her former school mate who worked there.

"Are you at work?"

"Yes, I'm in the back office."

"I'm in the line, meet me at the side."

Jessica saw her friend Charlie exiting the door

marked Office. She met him at the side counter.

"Hey hunny," she hugged him as she greeted him. "I need this prescription filled urgently."

He outstretched his hand and took the prescription, he looked at it and his eyes widened and flew to her stomach and up to meet her eyes. She nodded. "Congratulations Jess."

"Thank you, can you hurry please, I've got to get back to work."

"Come to the next window." He returned inside and sat behind the counter, he peeped at the prescription and started pulling boxes from shelves above him containing her prenatal vitamins. "So, how is married life?" Charlie had attended both her birthday dinner and wedding. They didn't chat everyday but they kept in touch with each other often.

"It's good. I have zero complaints."

"You must be doing something right if you're pregnant already," he scoffed.

"You need to mind the business that pays you," she chuckled.

"I am sweetheart." He then placed both prescriptions on the counter and gave her the total. She handed him one hundred dollars plus a tip. "Ooohhh, a generous tip, it must be my lucky day," he said in a very sarcastic manner.

"Thank you Charlie. Lunch is on me." She plucked

the vitamins from the counter and dropped them into her purse and blew a kiss at Charlie and walked to the carpark. She returned to work and took a break to take her recommended two pills with a bottle of water. She opened her laptop and graded Pamela's first showing. The details she entered were sent directly to her boss' email address and the company database. Pamela did pretty well and Jessica graded her accordingly.

Jessica spent the rest of the day doing her quarterly reports. She spoke with Trey briefly before finishing up for the day. At 4:00 p.m., she was out through the door. She stopped at the grocery store and picked up a few items for dinner later that night. She reached home and lugged her groceries inside, setting them on the counter; she walked back to the door and kicked off her shoes. Before she started dinner, she bathed and added a light gloss to her lips and eyeliner. She returned to the kitchen and began chopping up the vegetables and meat she purchased. Between peeling the sweet potatoes and whipping up a pan of delicious apple pie, she was sipping a cold glass of red wine. She switched the stove on and sautéed one onion and sweet pepper into her frying pan before adding her other vegetables and meat. Next she added her special sauces and herbs.

Trey entered as soon as she was finishing up dinner, she set the table and plated their food. He kissed her gently on her cheek and dashed up the stairs to freshen up. He returned and poured himself a glass of wine and bottle water for Jessica. She sucked her teeth when she saw the water but smiled inwardly. During dinner, Jessica handed Trey the photo from her ultrasound. He stopped chewing his vegetables and glared at the photo, intrigued.

"We should frame this?"

"I guess we can."

"This little speck could be our baby."

"Yip". She didn't need the 'could' reminder.

Jessica spent the rest of dinner informing a very attentive Trey what she went through at her doctor's visit.

"Damn, I'm sorry I missed it," he said.

"It was crazy seeing the little bud on the screen, I was kinda happy," she gushed.

For those few minutes sitting at dinner, there was no thought of any paternity issues or drama with her ex. All of their focus on was the baby growing in her stomach.

6

Over the next two months, Jessica could no longer hide her protruding stomach. After her second prenatal visit she finally told her boss that she was pregnant. She was aware of the subtle projection of her tummy when she wore anything fitted, it would not have been long before tongues started wagging, she also noticed that her underwear no longer fit her like before and her breasts were bigger and hurt like hell. She loved when Trey rubbed her swollen tummy, he was amazed watching her tummy swell and settle back down as the baby kicked or stretched. At 5 months pregnant, he or she moved around a lot, sometimes causing her slight pain. Thankfully, she suffered no morning sickness and she took her prenatal vitamins faithfully.

Jessica did a lot of baby shopping during her lunch breaks; she bought several varieties of shoes, socks and toys and several sets of unisex clothing since she didn't know the sex of the baby, her doctor did advise her that she was well at the mark to find out if she wanted too. On this particular Friday, she visited a more expensive baby store, one her sister Olivia referred her to. She did see a gorgeous cradle but she was not willing to pay over $1,000.00 for no damn crib. Olivia must be out her damn mind! She left the store empty handed and as she unlocked her door she noticed a familiar face in the car parked not far from hers.

"Timothy!" she shouted. He turned in the direction of the female voice. Timothy was one of her failed relationships. She came to the realization soon after their breakup that it just wasn't meant to be, they were quite young at the time. However, they had remained friendly and he was the only ex that she still communicated with.

"Jessica!" he got out of his car to greet her and they embraced quickly, "I can see how you are. Girl, what the hell!"

"Things change I guess." She laughed at his shocked expression.

"I bet they do. How is Trey?"

"He's great, really great."

"I bet he's super excited about being a father."

Jessica prayed that he didn't notice the change in her face and she smiled even harder. She let the comment sail away with the wind.

"What are you doing all the way over here?" she asked.

"My sister asked me to pick up an order for her from this expensive ass baby store. You know how you women are."

"Melanie is pregnant? I haven't seen her in forever."

"Melanie *had* her baby," he corrected her, "A sweet little princess."

"That's wonderful, tell her I said congrats."

"Yuh know, that could have been us.

"Okkk, so enjoy the rest of your day." She turned on her heels, heading back to her car.

"Wait, wait Jessica." He grabbed her arm and doubled over laughing. She also started laughing.

"That was so not cool." They were both still laughing. "I'm done with this convo, fuh real. I'm gonna go back to work and forget to you said that."

"Ok, I admit, that was a bit shady," he stopped and looked her up and down.

"You look really good, baby and all." A look of regret flashed across his face.

"Thanks Timothy," she felt uncomfortable,

"Anyway I've got to go. See you around."

"Yea, cool." He watched her walked back to her car and drove off. He sat in his car and remembered the fun times they had. He shook his head and went on his way.

Jessica picked up lunch on her way back to the office and ate while browsing the internet for boys' and girls' names. She couldn't really decide, so she wrote a few on a notepad to discuss with Trey later. Her boss called and asked her to present her quarterly report which she had been working on at a meeting in an hour so she was forced to quit her online search and get right to work. She made quick notes on her laptop and pulled up her four design charts and by the time the meeting was called, she was well prepared. Fifteen minutes later, she had presented a through report to the management team. After the meeting she returned to her online searches.

When she got home that evening, Trey was moving the baby items she had stashed in the office to the second bedroom of the house, which was being turned into the baby's room. The office was filled with boxes upon boxes, there was hardly any room on the desk to do any type of work. Trey had even come across wedding gift boxes that Jessica somehow had stored away in her office cabinets, he assumed because they were pretty.

"Please tell me you didn't buy anything else."

Jessica felt a sudden flutter in her tummy and she absentmindedly rubbed the area where she felt the spasm.

"Nope. I checked on the cribs today, it was a waste of my damn gas and time. It was too expensive but it was soooo gorgeous, look, I took a pic to show you."

He came over and looked at the photo, "That's dope."

"Yea, it is."

"How much money are you spending buying all this baby stuff Jess?"

"Money is no option baby."

"Ok ma'am."

"Listen, I have a job to check on so I'mma head out soon."

"I'm gonna go soak for a min. Just lock the door when you leave."

"Gotcha baby."

Jessica went into her bedroom and changed into her robe. She ran her bath water while she removed her makeup with baby wipes and she scooped her hair into a loose high bun. Once the tub was filed, she hung her robe on the hook behind the door and slid into the lukewarm water. Since becoming pregnant, she no longer enjoyed sitting in the extremely hot water. It made her nauseous and heated after and she found it hard to fall asleep when it was time for bed. She stiffened against a sharp kick, right in her side; she poured the warm water over her big belly and drew small circles on her skin with the droplets of water that remained.

Trey parked outside of an empty house, an hour away from home. He got out of his car and walked up to the door. He unlocked it and stepped in. He scanned the rooms adjacent the foyer. He figured one could be his office and the other his own personal bar. He walked to the back of the house, where he found a reasonably sized kitchen, he would definitely have to replace the outdated stove and refridgerator. He inspected the three giant bedrooms, the guest bathroom and the two fully equipped en suite bathrooms. He turned the electricity on and also checked the water pressure. He shook the frames around the doors, peeked into cupboards and cabinets, mentally taking note of what would need replacing. Trey was familiar with this house. He had spent many summers there as a young boy when he had visited with his uncle and his wife. The house was for sale and he was interested in purchasing it.

Jessica made sure she kept up with her appointments and taking her vitamins. At her sixth month doctor visit, she was walking slower than she was before; it took her at least two extra minutes to walk into the doctor's office. Her back hurt like a bitch and her nipples were sore against the fabric of her bra. The baby was developing superbly and she was managing all her aches and pains effortlessly, considering. She paid for her visit and made her way back to her car, en route to work. Jessica was in no way prepared for what happened next; as she pulled into her company's carpark, there was Ron sitting on the hood of his car. Jessica was stunned, she almost crashed her own damn car into the curb; she jerked to a halt, a disturbing thought filtered into her mind; she'd run him over with her car and tell the police she lost control. That would take care of her problem once and for all. If he was dead, uhmmm, the thought was delicious to her very soul.

Instead, she pulled into her designated spot and stepped out of her car.

"Hello Jessica." His cheery greeting instantly irritated the hell out of her.

"What the fuck do you want Ron?"

"Is that my baby you're carrying?"

"Negro, you must be out your damn mind, did I call and tell you that?"

"I didn't think you would, but from my own calculations, you might very well be."

"What the fuck is wrong with you? Do you get a rise from harassing pregnant women bitch?" Jessica was too pissed to remember the plan she and Charmaine had cooked up for Ron; forget being cordial and nice, he had her all the way fucked up.

"I need a DNA test, you can't keep me out of my child's life."

"I think you need to get the hell out of my face." And with that she turned and walked away.

"I'm serious, I would hate to get the law involved Jessica." He shouted at her back.

Once she hit the top of the steps, she looked back at Ron and flipped him the bird. He let out a cynical snort as she disappeared inside.

Jessica was pissed with herself for not following the plan, now he knew how to get under her skin. She earnestly regretted not plowing through him with her car. The bitch deserved it. Concentrating on work after her verbal altercation with Ron was impossible. She pushed her papers away and rested her head on her desk, she felt her baby shifting uncomfortably in her tummy so she sat upright in her chair.

If Ron was this annoying now, imagine if he turned out to be the father, he would be a nightmare to deal with, she cursed the day she met him at that party, she would have saved herself much heartache. Whelp! She was done giving him anymore of her energy. She waddled to the lunchroom and grabbed a bottled water from the refridgerator, sipping it slowly until her thirst was sated.

She ended her work day an hour early and kicked her heels off as soon as she got home. She felt sticky and hot. She pulled everything off except her bra and panties. She switched the tv on and sat on the throw she had spread across the couch. She made a quick trip to the refridgerator to grab a fruit salad, Trey had prepared for her that morning. Just before he was to arrive home, she showered and dressed in shorts and a loose top. Hopefully, she would be cool and not overly hot. Within seconds, her breasts ached terribly and she was forced to slip into a bra to help support her heavy breasts. Breasts secured, she sat waiting patiently for Trey to come home.

When she heard his car pull up, she rushed to the door and opened it before he could place his key in the lock. She rushed at him and wrapped her arms around him, he hugged her back and then stepped away to look at her.

"What's wrong?"

"Ron came to my workplace today."

She felt his body go rigid. "What did he say?"

She placed her hand in his closed the door and guided him to the couch.

"He was his usual annoying arrogant self."

"What did you say?"

"It didn't go anywhere as planned. I lost it

completely."

"Jessss, you know you can't egg him on, just ignore him, don't give into his bullshit."

"In my defense I really tried."

"Listen, I was doing some research and we can do the DNA test before the baby is born.

Jessica was taken aback. "Why were you researching early detection DNA tests?" she felt like he'd just punched her in the stomach, knocking the wind from her body.

"Then we can know before the baby is born. It's non-invasive, you'll only have to provide a blood sample."

Reality set in, "You'll never see me the same will you, whether this baby is yours or Ron's."

"What are you talking about?" he was utterly confused.

Honestly Jessica didn't know what the hell she was talking about either, she was just upset about what he had said, she was annoyed and frustrated, she wasn't ready to find out yet, she simply wanted to go on thinking her baby was Trey's.

Jessica got up from the couch, plucking her keys from the counter without a word to Trey, she slammed the front door shut and climbed into her car. She sat there, her minded urging her to... just drive.

7

They hardly spoke to each other the next morning, when she'd return later that night, Trey was pretending to be asleep. She was thankful, she did not want to speak to him. She had to face the fact that the pressure of him not knowing who she was pregnant for, was taking a toll on him, he hardly touched her growing bump; he probably didn't want to get attached to a baby that potentially might not be his. She wasn't upset with him, she was saddened that he was unable to enjoy the experience as he would have if there was no doubt of paternity.

Jessica parked in her appointed work spot and tossed her purse and work bag over her shoulders from the back seat, as she stepped out of her car, her breathing was labored, the more her baby grew, the harder she fought to breathe. The maternity clothing she'd bought for this exact occasion were feeling a little snug over her baby bump.

"Good Morning Syl," she said sweetly.

"Good Morning, mommy- to- be. There's a package on your desk which I signed for this morning."

"Thanks hun." As soon as she saw the bouquet of flowers on the desk, she knew they were from Ron. He'd sent her those very roses during their relationship. She plucked the card from the stick and read the note... Ron and Jessica were kissing in a tree, k...i...s...s...i...n...g...Jessica fucked the entire bouquet in the trash. What an asshole.

Just then, Bryan popped his head through her open door.

"You look swell today," he broke out in all loud roar.

"You're in the wrong field Bryan, that little quip was outstanding. I mean I can hardly contain myself," She kept her head down, rolling her eyes hard as hell.

"Yea. Yea. Cyrus wants you to handle these and get them back to him in 48 hours, his words not mine."

Jessica breathed deeply through her nose. Her boss had no idea the kind of stress she was under already.

"He's Cyrus now eh," she smiled.

"Between us, he's Cyrus, between him and I, he's boss," he corrected her.

"Thanks, I'll take a look at them later."

He left as fast as he had come.

Her office line rang again.

"Hello. This is Jessica Sommers!"

"I take it you got my gift."

"You're free to come stick them up your ass."

"Did you like my little nursery rhyme?"

Jessica slammed the phone down in his ear, she made a promise to herself to not let him raise her blood pressure.

She started picking through the paperwork Bryan dumped on her. She was ready for maternity leave. Her cell chirped.

"Hi."

"I'm sorry about last night," Trey said, "this is harder than I thought it would be."

"I know."

"I'm gonna make it up to you later, I promise."

"You don't have to Trey, I'm fine."

"See you at home later?"

"Sure thing baby!" She hung up and returned to her papers.

Jessica was bombarded by calls and emails, she never got a break until two in the afternoon, she barely had time to snack on a couple orange slices she brought from home and bottled water. The constant need to use the bathroom was the most annoying part of her pregnancy. She was fed up of it all and swiftly told her boss she was leaving early.

At home she found Max asleep in his bed, she refilled his bowls and went to take a nap in her bed. Again, she stripped to her bra and panties, she was asleep as soon as her head hit the pillow. A swift jolt in her abdomen, jumped her from her sleep. She could no longer lie on her back so she shifted from her right side to her left. She patted her extremely distended stomach and instantly, her baby moved at the movement of her hand. She plugged her headphones into her cell and stretched them across her tummy, she played a soothing instrumental she found online, this was to help babies to relax in the womb, a tidbit she found while browsing the internet.

Apparently she had fallen back to sleep when her cell rang, she removed the headphones and answered.

"I've petitioned the court for a DNA test."

"Aren't you supposed to be recovering from soft tissue damage instead of being a pain in my ass?" she asked sharply.

"You know I stay hard all night baby!" Jessica ended the call and blocked that number immediately.

Now, she'd never get back to sleep. She dwelled on the conversation she had with Trey bout early testing.

She was deathly scared to do it, she thought she could delay the testing until after the baby was born. She stayed in bed until Trey came home later in the evening from work and while he ate she dialed her parents, they were both were concerned with her well-being now that she was heavily pregnant.

"Jessica, I am serious you need to slow down."

"Mum, I'm ok. I'll stop working maybe a month before I'm due to deliver.

"You never listen!" her father intervened.

"Listen to what daddy. My doctor said I can work until I'm ready to go on maternity leave."

"I gave Charmaine some items I bought for the baby, has she given you yet?"

"She told me, she's to bring them over at some point."

"Is the baby a boy or girl?" Her mother asked excitedly.

"I have no idea, mummy. I haven't done the ultrasound as yet."

"What are you waiting for?"

"I'm not sure I want to know, I can wait, it'll be a sweet surprise for Trey and I."

Trey came into the room soon after, since Jessica was on the phone he headed back downstairs.

"I've got to talk to Trey, I'll shout you guys back."

"Ok hunny! Have a good night," they said.

Jessica was very careful when taking the stairs. She eventually made it down to the landing where she found Trey ruffling Max's fur. "Hey baby. I was just gonna take Max for a walk. How are you feeling?"

"I could be better, big belly and all," she said jokingly.

Jessica was still in her bra and panties. She was still very sexy to him even with her huge belly. Her body seemed curvier and her breasts heavy laden with milk were perfectly plump. He loved the way they felt in his hands. He felt the sudden spasm of his building erection. They had sex, yes, but it was nowhere close to the wild romps they relished in before she found out she was pregnant. He hardly played with her stomach, he wanted to but he always changed his mind at the last second. She sat next to him on the couch, her heels resting on the coffee table. He tentatively stroked her moving belly with one finger. She looked at him surprised.

With enough courage, he gently palmed her entire belly, the baby somersaulted causing Jessica to wince in pain.

He jerked his hand back "I'm sorry, was I too rough?"

"No, that was just a big ass kick."

"What does that feel like?" he was still palming her stomach as the baby pushed up against his warm hand.

"Hmmm, it feels like I got stabbed in my guts."

"Damn, that's no joke"

He continued rolling his hand all over her stomach, delighted in feeling the baby push against his palm. Even though he preferred to have the early DNA test done, he had decided not to pressure her to have the blood work done, he was prepared to wait it out. Coincidentally she mentioned it to him.

"Ron wants me to have that early DNA thing you were telling me about."

"Where did you see him to discuss that?"

"He keeps sending me flowers with silly notes concerning my pregnancy."

"Are you gonna do it?"

"I might do it just to get him out of my butt."

"I'll support you no matter your decision."

"Thank you," she was honestly grateful for his support.

Trey's hooked his fingers in the top of her panties, he ran his hand over the ribbed top of her undies and slid his hand straight down her panties, cupping her crotch in his hand.

"I need to shower," she said as he continued stroking the lips of her slit, soaking his fingers with her wetness.

"No you don't," he pulled his hand out and marveled at the thick liquid dripping from his fingertips. He sucked his fingertips dry, he wanted to have her right then. "Turn around for me baby." He helped her off the couch and she positioned herself gently on her knees into the soft cushions of the couch. He pulled her panties down to her knees and dropped his boxers to the floor. He rubbed his engorged shaft head between her shaved slit, pushing her silky lips apart, before sinking into her wetness. Jessica moaned softly as he filled her to the hilt.

"Damn baby," He carefully pumped into her from behind. Trey leaned his head back, pouring all his frustrations into the cavern between her legs, her pregnancy made her even sweeter and her walls felt slick like oil, he felt her muscles tighten and pull him in deeper, driving him over the edge, he trembled violently as he drained his entire load into her. "Oohh shit Jess", he melded into her, his body jerking with each shot of his release. He flopped on the couch with her still bent over. She pulled her panties up and shifted gently to her butt.

Jessica lifted her legs one by one over his naked thighs, cum was still oozing from his shaft. She rubbed her stomach since the baby didn't seem to delight in the interference it was subjected to.

"Let's go shower," he said. He helped her from the couch and guided her up the stairs to the bathroom. They took turns washing each other's bodies thoroughly before returning to the bedroom to snuggle in the bed. By 9:00 p.m. she was out cold while Trey sat in the bed with his laptop going over architectural plans.

8

That Friday, when she entered her office, there on her desk, sat another bouquet of flowers and a note. She was hesitant to read the note, she peeked at it, 'Mummy's baby....Daddy's maybe.' Jessica ripped the note in half and tossed the roses into the thrash. Ron was living up to being a pain where she didn't need any pain.

Jessica sat, breathing slowly and deeply, she was desperately trying not to lose her shit over Ron, but he persisted in harassing her. She even stopped telling Trey about her encounters with Ron. If he wasn't calling her from unknown numbers, he was sending roses to her office with stupid notes attached. He obviously knew not to send them to her house. She wondered where the man she fell in love with had disappeared to, he obviously was not a part of the Ron she was currently dealing with. She prayed he would leave her alone. But as usual, her prayers were never answered.

"Why are you denying me the right to know whether I'm going to be a father again?"

"I'm not denying you anything. I wish you'd stop playing with me, stress isn't good for a pregnant woman." She gasped as a sudden pressure quickened across her mid-section.

"What choice do I have? You ignore me completely."

Jessica decided to try a different approach. "When the baby is born, I'll have the DNA test done."

There was silence. "If the baby's mine, I will be filing for 50/50 custody."

"Nothing else would be surprise." Jessica rolled her eyes so hard, her eyebrows twitched for a couple seconds after. "I would really appreciate your cooperation here."

"Fine, I will wait until the baby is born, but bear in mind Jessica, if you're carrying my baby...mmm. We'll just wait and see. Do you remember how badly you wanted to have my children? *He might not come when you want him but he's always on time.*" All she heard was raucous laughter, as she slammed the phone into its cradle on her desk. Jessica could not listen to him for one more second. She hated him with everything in her. She prayed that she didn't have to deal with him for eighteen years.

She was determined to have the last laugh. Little did they all know that she had given her doctor a sample of her blood and a sample of Trey's hair that she yanked from his head while he was dead asleep one night, he hardly acknowledged the pain, he simply rolled over on his side. The truth of her baby's paternity was hidden in a sealed white envelope, locked away in a drawer in her home office, she didn't have the courage to open the envelope just yet.

Jessica was now eight months pregnant. She had one more month to go before delivering her baby. If she was walking slowly at seven months, she was moving at a snail's pace at eight months. She felt like a freight train, her abdomen was huge and her breasts swollen and tender, she no longer could see her toes and Trey was now her groomer, he gladly lotioned her swollen feet and impressively assisted in her daily chores and took very good care of her. He cooked, cleaned and did all of the laundry except the baby clothing. He left that to her.

Jessica discussed with her boss, her working from home; he agreed and she spent her last week in the office. She had stopped receiving bouquets from Ron, she guessed her plea for cooperation got through to him.

The files she brought home were tossed unceremoniously on the coffee table in the living room, where she now spent most of her days. It seemed the final days of her pregnancy were moving at warp speed. At her last prenatal visit, she openly asked her doctor's advice on obtaining a paternity test as soon as the baby was born. She knew both Trey and Ron were desperate for answers.

Being at home and being catered to by Trey, was one of the perks of being pregnant she enjoyed the most, he was literally at her beck and call, she was only alone when he had to go to his office and even then he'd call her every hour to ensure she and the baby were okay. Jessica shrieked as a sharp pain radiated from her pubic bone to her ribs. She sat back against the couch cushions, waiting for the pain to subside. She was experiencing excruciating pain around her uterus since entering her third trimester, her doctor told her it was most likely Braxton Hicks contractions, which was a simulation of labour pains and her body preparing for delivery.

Jessica heard when she pulled up and parked outside.

"Jess, where you at?" Charmaine slipped the extra key Jessica gave her into her pants pockets as she entered. She came over once every week to supply Jessica with fruits and any cravings she asked her to bring when she came.

"Living room!" Jessica shouted back.

"I couldn't find the chocolate you wanted so I got you some Cadbury."

"I don't eat Cadbury chocolate?"

"Well you gonna eat it today," she snapped.

Jessica snatched the chocolate from Charmaine's outstretched hand and opened the candy bar.

"Anymore roses from Ron?"

"Not one."

"How long do you think that will last?"

Jessica shrugged and popped one of the squared bars into her mouth. She was ready for her pregnancy to be over. Her sex life had slowed tremendously, intercourse became more uncomfortable the further along she got and she was constantly hot and irritated and her body ached in places that never ached before. "I hope forever."

"You look tired and fat."

Jessica swatted her sister across her arms as they

were on the couch chatting.

"I feel fat as hell, I don't even wear panties anymore but I have to stay in a bra, my boobs swell as soon as I take it off."

"Welcome to motherhood sissy."

"I was in no way ready to be a parent; I always planned to have kids maybe three years after I got married. Now, I can't wait to meet him or her," she gushed.

"How does Trey feel?"

Jessica's demeanor saddened. "He's changed, he's probably touched my stomach about once or twice, I know he's trying not to bond with the baby in case it's not his. I mean I get it. Honestly Char, if he leaves and I'm in no way being a bitch..., he leaves. I'm tired of apologizing for sleeping with Ron. It's either he accepts my apology or he doesn't."

"Jess, you can't hurt a person and then tell them how long it takes them to get over it. Believe me, I one hundred percent understand where you are coming from, but girl, you are a *married* pregnant woman, who doesn't know whose her child's father, that's not something easy to deal with."

"I know." Jessica felt like a heathen, she looked away briefly. She hated when Charmaine watched her too closely gauging her reactions.

"What are you going to do if he leaves?"

"I'm going to raise my child alone."

"That's not as easy as it sounds Jess."

"I'll do whatever I have to do." She was resolute in her position. She was no longer going to beg Trey to stay with her. She had done the damage so she'd have to deal with the consequences of her actions.

"Well you know, I'll always be here for you and your baby."

"Thank you."

"I've got to run, I'm driving car-pool today and Tai and Demarco have swim practice later in the evening and I don't want to be late."

"Thanks for swinging by."

"I'll call you later tonight."

Once alone, she began to cry. Crying for so many different reasons, she was unsure which issue bugged her the most, they were all jumbled together into a large ball of shit. A nagging feeling crept up her spine... the envelope. She was home alone. She had the perfect opportunity to read the contents. Not knowing was eating her alive, she wanted to know but mentally she was exhausted. Instead, she pulled her laptop out and responded to several work related emails. Her eyes bulged when she saw there was an email from Ron. She deleted it swiftly.

She paused, thinking. She heaved and struggled to get off of the couch, she entered her office and went straight to the shelves elevated on one end of her office wall, she lifted one of the decorative ornaments from the shelf and removed the key to the locked drawer and sat in her office chair. She unlocked the drawer and removed the white envelope. She balanced it on the edge of the desk, which barely had any room, it was overflowing with baby items still in their boxes. Jessica had to hold her hand steady with her other hand, it was trembling wildly, "Just breathe baby", she ripped opened the envelope with her nails and pulled the sheet of paper out, it was folded in half.

"Jess!"

Shit, fuck. Trey was home. She hastily stuffed the sheet of paper back into the envelope and back into the drawer, she relocked the drawer and slipped the key into her bra just as Trey appeared at her office door.

"What are you doing?"

"I was thinking of sorting all of this baby stuff I have stored in here." She tapped on the boxes crowding the desk.

"Cool, do you need any help?"

"Nope, I'll leave that for tomorrow, how was your day?"

"It was pretty decent; no stress, no problems, I need more of these days actually."

"Are you hungry, we have some left overs, I can heat up for you?"

"Nahhhh, maybe I'll eat something later. Join me on the couch for a moment."

Jessica carefully eased her heavy butt from the chair. She waddled into the living room and Trey helped her down into the couch.

"You are so big baby, damn." He chuckled. Jessica squinted at him and smacked him hard against his thigh. "I didn't mean it in a bad way, you are all belly."

"I am with child, what did you expect," she scoffed.

He pulled both of her legs onto his thighs and began rubbing her feet. She was in heaven. She adjusted the pillows behind her back and enjoyed the pressure at the bottom of her feet. She read somewhere that massaging a pregnant woman's feet was unhealthy, she couldn't remember, but she felt so relaxed she begged him not to stop.

"The baby's room is almost complete. During this week I'm going to move the boxes from the office to the bedroom, it'll be easier for you to arrange the room however you like, did you remember to order the chest?"

"Thank you and no, I forgot. I'll have to do that tomorrow too."

As Trey returned to rubbing her feet, it dawned on her that she needed to get the envelope out of her office as soon as possible.

9

By the time Trey went to shower, Jessica was frantically removing the folded sheet of paper from the white envelope. She read the contents quickly, her heart was beating out of her mouth, she read it slower the second time, not comprehending the words fully, but taking mental snap shots of the individual letters and percentage noted on the sheet. She stepped out of the office, straining to hear whether the shower was still running. She flicked the stove on and placed the end of the sheet into the fire, as the bright flame spread across the paper she dropped it into the sink. When the sheet was nothing but blackened ash, she washed the contents down the sink and pulled a tissue from the holder on the Island and wiped her forehead. She also wiped the interior of the sink, removing any remaining ash residue.

"Oh my God!" Her stomach bubbled, forcing the contents of her guts into the sink she had just cleaned. She released the sprayer and washed the bottom of sink until she could see the stainless steel bottom, her baby moved restlessly, hurling more of her stomach contents into the sink.

"Hey, Hey, Hey, are you sick?"

She felt her body swaying, Trey scooped her up and rested her on the couch. He ran into the kitchen and returned with a soaked kitchen towel, which he gently placed on her forehead.

"Do you want to go to the hospital?"

"No," she managed. "Think I ate something that made me throw up." When did she become a scheming liar, she thought.

"Are you sure?" His face was a mask of concern. "Do you want me to call Charmaine?"

"No. I want to go to bed."

"Ok." He eased her legs off the couch and lifted her to the bedroom and she lay on top of the covers. "I'll go get you a bottled water." He bounded down the stairs and was back before she knew it. He stood above her, observing her every breath.

"Trey I'm fine, it was just bad food."

"Are you sure?"

"Yes, can you find the tv remote?"

Trey tousled the covers and found the remote beneath his pillow.

"Here," he said handing her the remote.

"I'm going to start bringing the boxes up from the office, if you need me just shout." She nodded as he pecked her on her cheek.

Jessica removed the kitchen towel from her forehead, resting it on the side table. She had to cry, her brain was in shock and her baby would not stop moving. Between the rolling in her head and the rolling in her tummy, she was a wreck. She couldn't form a complete sentence if her life depended on it. There had to be something she could do to get her out of her predicament. But what? She placed a pillow at her back and one between her knees.

Trey repeatedly checked in on her while he moved all of the boxes into the baby's room, he was extremely vigilant and came running at the slightest noise coming from the bedroom. Whenever he peeked in on her, she felt worse and worse, tears soaked her pillow as she tried crying silently, sniffling ever so slightly so he wouldn't hear her.

She was aware that once Trey found out she was pregnant with Ron's baby, he would leave her. She couldn't let that happen, she had to find a way to alter this highway to hell. She refused to raise a child with Ron, she'd rather pull her toenails out with a pliers. She ached for a glass of wine, her nerves were fried and she needed to relax. Since she couldn't have wine, there was only one other option.

"Trey!"

He appeared at the door, "Yeah," he was sweating lightly from the several treks up and down the stairs. She signaled him over with her index finger, she gingerly switched to her back as he stood over her.

"I need you to do something for me." She seductively spread her legs and he read her signal loud and clear. Jessica rubbed her clit with one finger, her body sensors instantly hummed as the memory of self-pleasure danced in her eyes.

"One second," she heard him say. When he returned his body was wet and he looked fresh; he'd taken a shower. He took over from Jessica and sucked on his own fingers before sliding two into her bit by bit. She was dripping by the time he removed his glistening fingers. He kneeled before her, gripping her thighs as he planted his tongue deep inside of her, some inaudible mumbo jumbo escaped her lips and after ten minutes, he withdrew his tongue and began lapping at her clit. Jessica gripped the covers of the bed, she bucked and gyrated her hips all over his firm tongue. This is exactly what she needed. A giant sexual release.

Within seconds, his tongue was drenched in her juices, he lapped at her slit faster and faster until she came, "Oh fuck Trey don't stop." A loud scream bubbled out of her as her climax rocked her whole body, Jessica's back was no longer on the bed, only her head, she felt as though she'd been electrocuted as her body quivered from the jolts traveled through her, even milk squirted from her nipples and trickled down the sides of her breasts.

Trey was so turned on, he licked the spilled milk from both breasts, he squeezed and sucked on her nipples sending her body into another spasm as a second orgasm sent her flying, she rubbed her clit vigorously as blinding lights appeared behind her closed eyes. "Turn on your side," he waited for her quivering to wane before asking her, she shifted to her side and he entered her gently, her walls greedily pulling him in as he glided in and out of her and he felt her juices trickling out of her onto his balls. Damn! He rested his head on her shoulder, stroking her carefully, he sensed the baby was pushing against his palm which was softly caressing her stomach. After six pumps he was losing it, it took all of his control not to fuck the shit out of her, he thrust into her as skillfully as he could without hurting her, her moans were low and contented when he finally released his seed deep inside of her.

70

It took him a while before he got his breathing under the control. Jessica was quiet next to him, he peeped over her shoulder to see her face. Fuck! She was asleep. Trey washed off in the bathroom, he was in awe at the amount of Jessica's juices still dripping from the tip of his wood. He returned to the bed and lay in front of her. He watched her sleep, upset that he could not give her one hundred percent of himself. He still loved her, that was true, but he was pulling away the closer she got to the end of her pregnancy.

Trey had purchased his uncle's home, the one he visited recently. He was able to purchase it at a steal; it required a little work but nothing he couldn't handle. He wanted to tell Jessica about it but he knew she wouldn't understand and he didn't want to stress her out now that she was so close to having the baby. He brushed a coily strand of hair from her face and kissed her lips lightly. As her husband, it was his duty to protect and care for her and it pissed him off totally that she'd probably never step foot in his new house with her new baby, he would have been overjoyed to raise their son or daughter in a home where he had such vivid and happy memories from his childhood.

He wondered for a moment whether she would eventually rekindle with Ron if he was her baby's father. The thought made him jump from the bed. He flung on a joggers pants bottom and went down the stairs. He took two beers from the refridgerator and stepped onto the patio. He gulped one beer in seconds, burped and popped the cap on the next. His mind was unsettled. He had confided in his brother Samuel that he and Jessica were having problems and not to tell their mother anything just yet.

He sat the bottle on the floor as a sleepy looking Max appeared at the open door. "Hey boy, did I wake you?" Trey patted Max's head and the dog stretched out in the doorway next to his feet. At some time during the night, he went to bed, now he couldn't sleep, his mind was racing, he took his phone from the night stand and started pulling up his personal house plans for the house on Carters Boulevard, he wanted to begin renovations soon, he'd order the lumber and his workmen were to begin demolishing the back structure, which needed reinforcement and he also made plans to have the pool area dug before he had to move out, well if it came to that.

He spent hours and hours going over his plans and making notes on the drawings. He finally fell asleep around 4:00 a.m. and Jessica was up an hour later. She slept so much better after she released the mounting tension she felt last night. The smile across her face disappeared as she recalled the reason for her tension. She let out an annoyed grunt which raised Trey from his slight sleep.

"Good Morning," he said.

"Hey sleepy head."

"You were out cold last night," he chuckled.

"Boy I needed that release," she laughed.

"What are your plans for today?"

"I want to go to the mall and that's about it."

"I thought you wanted to stop driving in case you go into labour?"

"Well do you want to drive me around today?"

"Just be careful on the road baby," they both laughed out loud, "call me if anything happens, ok?"

Jessica flipped him the piece sign.

Trey left the bedroom, to go start breakfast, he would leave hers in the microwave until she came down to eat. Jessica sat up and used her arms to lift her body against the headboard. She didn't want to think about the obvious, Ron was her baby's father, she had to get in front of it before the baby was born. When Trey left for work, she headed downstairs, her breakfast was still slightly warm so she set it on the island and dialed her Attorney.

Within an hour, she was seated before Sara, her Attorney.

"Hi Sara, thanks for seeing me on such short notice." They were on a first name basis, it made certain situations easier to discuss.

"What's so urgent that you had to see me right

away?"

Jessica needed to choose her words carefully, "I need you to draw up a concrete parenting Agreement for me."

"Why?" She asked sipping on her coffee.

"I'm not pregnant with my husband's baby," her tone unwavering. Hot coffee shot out of Sara's mouth, sprinkling directly onto Jessica's chest.

"I'm so sorry Jessica," she said genuinely. She handed her a tissue from the holder on her desk. "I don't know what to say, does Trey know?"

Jessica waved her apology away, "Actually, Ron is the father."

Sara didn't bat an eye. "That would explain a lot." She rubbed her chin before proceeding, "I saw Ron some time ago and he made certain innuendos about you and him but it wasn't my place to question you about them."

"Oohhh that son of a bitch," she whispered.

They discussed the terms of the agreement and ground rules she needed Ron to abide by, visitation and child support.

"I'll draft the agreement and send it to you within a few days. Jessica, I must warn you, he's not a fair player; he prides himself on being a brutal investment banker, it's his job to win. If I may be frank, I think he's still in love with you, from my short interaction with him, he's upset that you moved on with Trey, it was like a slap in his face, I believe he wanted you to stay with him while he handled his issues with Lydia and the kids."

"In all honesty Sara, that wasn't going to happen." Jessica took her bag loosely by the handles preparing to leave. "Thank you Sara." She hefted her body from her chair and gradually strolled back to her car. She spotted Ron eagerly walking towards her.

"Well hello Mrs. Sommers, it's so lovely to see you," he greeted her.

Silence.

"I must say you are looking absolutely breathtaking," he sighed.

She got into her car and closed the door, it snagged against Ron's hand as he held it firmly. She looked up at him, squinting against the sun. "Will you and the husband be moving into his new home on Carters Boulevard? It is a beautiful property isn't it? He saw the look of confusion dart across her face. "I assumed you knew. Well, have a wonderful day Mrs. Sommers." He removed his hand from her door and she slammed it shut and locked her doors. She watched him strut away confidently.

She needed to get rid of Ron once and for all. With him out of the way she would convince Trey there was no need for a damn DNA test.

10

Jessica pulled up to her curb, she took her cell out and punched in a number.

"Hey, how are you?" She smiled. "I need you to do me a favour, check on the owner of Lot 6 Carters Boulevard, it's in St. James and I need the info back today. Thanks, I owe you one." She ended the call.

Why would Trey buy the house in Carters and not tell her about it. She knew it was the house he spent many summers with his uncle but it didn't make sense. Then it hit her, he was preparing to move after the baby was born. What was he going to do if the baby was his; expect her to pack up and move to Carters? Her baby rolled and kicked her right between her legs. She winced as the pain ricocheted up her back. She quickly spread her legs wider hoping that would ease the discomfort between her legs.

Jessica was now nine months and three days

pregnant. Her stomach protruded so far out she kept bouncing it against items in the house and the Braxton Hicks contractions were worst each time they started. She literally kept a diary to track and monitor her contraction times as they progressed. She cautiously took the stairs to her room and showered, she felt totally disgusted and every crevice of her body seemed to sweat or store heat. When she was finished she gently patted her stomach and dressed in one of Trey's shirts, they were the only clothing that fit comfortably.

She adjusted the pillows in the bed before gingerly climbing onto it. She raised her shirt and played with her tummy, she sang to her baby, who pushed and turned in her stomach. Jessica was fascinated by the awkward angles her stomach made as the baby stretched out or moved. She took quick photos on her phone. She thought of sending them to Trey but he probably wouldn't have even said anything. He was still distant towards her as far as the baby was concerned.

Jessica ordered lunch and sat waiting for her food to arrive, she signed into Google Earth and typed in the address for Carters Boulevard, as she waited for the page to load, she checked her cell to see if her contact had messaged her. Finally, the photos popped up and she felt her chest tighten. There was construction going on the property, there was lumber stacked to one side and she also saw the beginnings of a pool at the back of the property. Hmmm. She exited the site. She blew air out of her mouth and leaned back against the couch.

She thought long and hard about Trey. He didn't deserve the sorrow she had dumped on top of his head. She loved him to the moon and back and she knew he loved her just as much, but, she was prepared to raise her baby without him, she had money and she had her own home, they would lack for nothing.

Charmaine came over at the same time her food arrived. She paid the driver and met Jessica at the door.

"Thanks."

"What's up?" she asked.

"Nothing, only tired and achy." Jessica did not reveal to Charmaine that she had a paternity test done and that she knew that Ron was her baby's father.

"It's about that time sissy, how are you sleeping?"

"That's a new word, I hardly get a full night's sleep."

"Hopefully he or she makes an appearance soon."

"Cheers to that!"

Jessica pulled the food container open, and the heat swirled and danced up into her face, she dug right in, Charmaine took a fork from the utensil drawer in the kitchen and sampled a small portion of the okra slush.

"Hmmm, this is delicious." She scooped up a tiny bit more.

"Stopppp." Jessica was no mood to share her food.

"Damn, you're selfish."

"Bleh."

Charmaine spent an hour with her sister before heading home.

"Do you need anything before I go?"

"Wanna give me a massage?"

"Nope. Let your man do that."

"Whateva."

Charmaine kissed her sister on her forehead. "Bye sister."

"Bye hun. Lock the door for me."

Jessica finished up her lunch and sat her laptop on her knees. She pulled up her work sheets and leafed through her several clients' accounts. She spent the next three hours updating and reviewing her work sheets and responding to emails. She also sent Sylvia and her boss requests for information on files she did not have access to at home. Jessica enjoyed working from home. The remote access would be a great advantage when her baby was born.

Trey came home around 3:00 p.m. and she felt a surge of anger when she looked at him.

"Hi baby," he kissed her full on her lips.

"Hey," she wanted to ask him about the house on Carters, but her contact still hadn't sent her anything yet. She had to wait.

"What did you do today?"

"Work mostly."

4

"Any more pain?"

"Yip. How was your day?" She glared at him, waiting for his answer.

"It dragged, it was shit no lie."

"Anything major happened?"

"Nah not really, tonight I have to finish up in the baby's room, the side walls I still have to paint and hang the curtains.

"Did you peek in?"

"Nope. You ask me not to look yet and I haven't, I swear."

"Good. I want it to be a surprise." Trey was out of his mind if he thought she was not going into the baby's room, keeping an eye on his progress.

"Did you look at the color schemes I sent you?"

"Yea, I love the sunflower yellow, it's beautiful."

"Perfect. I'll order it and get my guys to paint the room over the weekend."

"That's great, the faster you get it done the better."

"Good, I'm gonna go get started."

"Cool. I'll watch tv down here for a while." Jessica relaxed on the couch and watched tv until she eventually drifted off to sleep. Charmaine slapped her on thigh. She opened her eyes to Charmaine, Olivia, Rebecca, Ashley and her parents standing around her.

She squealed out loud. "What are you guys doing here?"

5

She slid forward and stood to greet her parents and her sisters.

"You didn't want a baby shower so we are having a baby gathering," Ashley said.

There were carrying gifts and balloons, wine, chocolates and food.

"Where's your husband?" her dad asked.

"He's upstairs in the baby's room."

"I'll leave you ladies to it then."

Jessica was elated to see her family.

"Guys, I feel like I'm going to cry." She kept fanning her face, blowing the tears away.

Her mother came over and caressed her pregnant belly. They decided to sit on the patio sharing food and wine and bouncing names for both boys and girls off of each other.

"Boy or girl? Olivia asked.

"Girl." Jessica said eagerly.

"What about Trey?"

She shared a quick glance with Charmaine, "He just wants a healthy baby," she said.

After about an hour of chatting and eating, Trey and her dad came onto the patio. Her mother poured both of them a glass of wine. Her cell chirped and she checked the display, it was the message from her contact. She read the message, her face remained emotionless as the words sunk in. She looked at Trey and he was watching her. She deleted the message and returned her phone to the table. She'd deal with him later.

"Thank you mum," Trey said.

"Are you ready to be a father Trey, the late nights, the lack of sleep, a crying screaming baby?" Rebecca teased.

"I got this girl," he laughed heartily.

"Jess, come look at this." Charmaine shouted from inside the house.

Jessica stepped into the living room and saw the beautiful cradle she had seen at the store on Meadow Lane. She walked over to it and trailed her fingers over the intricately designed carvings on the sides of the white painted cradle. There were four drawers at the bottom to hold the essentials the baby would need at hand.

"It's so beautiful guys. Thank you so much," she wiped tears away from her eyes, as fresh droplets rolled out nonstop.

"You're welcome baby," her mum said.

"We were happy to purchase it for you," Olivia said teary eyed.

While the ladies returned to mingling among each other, Trey and her dad struggled to get the heavy cherry wood cradle up the stairs. By 10:00 p.m. Jessica was feeling tired. Charmaine picked up on it and covertly wrapped up the evening. She took the trash out after they tidied up and Jessica walked them to the door.

She hugged her parents goodbye and wished them all safe trips home.

Back inside, Trey was leaning on the kitchen island. She stretched her hand out, "Ready for bed?" he took her hand, "Ever since," she chuckled as she cautiously went up the stairs to their bedroom. Trey flipped the lights off and helped her under the covers. As soon as he heard her light snore, he rolled over backing her, eyes wide open.

11

Jessica awoke that Monday morning in immense pain, she immediately called her doctor, who instructed her to get to the hospital once her contractions were five minutes apart. Trey stood watching here, she would later remember him sweating profusely and biting his nails. He helped her into the shower, she started to lather quickly before the next contraction came, Jessica knees grew weak as the next contraction ripped through her stomach and she clenched her teeth against the intense pain. She leaned against the wall of the shower as tears spilled down her cheeks.

Trey noticed her slipping slightly so he stepped in

clothes and all to hold her upright.

"I'm ok," she said in a hushed tone. She washed the soap from her body and he then helped her to step out of the shower stall. She walked sluggishly back to her bed where Trey placed a towel beneath her to help soak up the water dripping off of her. She stuffed all of the pillows on the bed behind her back which was aching terribly.

"I need the pink and blue dress from over the closet door."

"This?"

"Yea," he handed her the dress, "Thanks," she snapped her bra and adjusted her breasts in the cups of the bra and brought the dress over her head.

"Why are you standing over there," the sight of him wet with his finger in his mouth sent her into fits of laughter. "Trey I'm fine."

"Is it time?"

"I think so."

He came over and embraced her. She let him hold her, it was the most genuine contact he'd had with her over the latter portion of her pregnancy. She rested her head next to his until his cold clothing prickled her skin.

"Change your clothes, baby, you're fricking me cold," she said. He kicked off his wet clothes and found a warm sweat shirt and matching pants.

Thankfully, her pains had subsided and she took a nap. Once she was asleep, Trey made her a small portion of scrambled eggs but he was too frazzled to eat it when he was finished, instead he woke her that she could eat to keep her strength up, he was sure she was going to need it soon. After eating, she went back to sleep for about fifteen minutes and Trey placed her bag and the baby's bag at the front door.

Trey sat in the living room, stressed, his new home was practically finished, he only had light cleaning to do and he intended to hire the same cleaning firm he used when he finished his business projects. His new home was fully furnished and the pool was due to be filled in the next two weeks. He felt burdened, he wasn't sure if he and his wife would ever live as a family in his home.

It scared him shitless seeing her in excruciating pain. He'd never seen a woman in labour before and he didn't want to see it again. All of his nails were bitten down to the nubs. He wished he could give her something to ease the pain of the contractions, but what? Anyway, he would soon know if her baby was his. The thought made his head hurt. If the baby wasn't his he would move out as soon as possible. He wanted to avoid seeing Ron too, his smug ass was sure to push him to do something he would regret.

At least, Jessica's sister and mother would be there for her. Her mother was scheduled to move in and he'd already set up an extra bed in the baby's room to accommodate her. Charmaine would obviously ensure she was okay if he left, he was certain of that fact but he would try to make the transition as smooth as possible. He would never leave her out of his life, he loved her and hopefully they could retain some semblance of a friendship.

He stretched out on the couch, his stomach felt a little hungry but his soul was aching.

Jessica finally woke from her nap. Her stomach felt hard and tight. She guessed Trey was downstairs or in the baby's room, she didn't get a chance to ask him about the house on Carters but she needed to know. Trey heard Jessica scream his name and he bounded up the steps two at a time, when he got into the bedroom, he was surprised, she looked relaxed.

"You bought the house on Carters?"

"Jess!" he was about to have a panic attack and she wanted to talk about his home, he was perplexed.

"This isn't the time," he said slowly.

"I only want to know why?"

"You know why."

"You could have told me." She felt the water settle in her eyes. He came and sat next to her.

"I'm sorry. I didn't want to hurt you, especially since you were pregnant.

"I'm going to miss you."

12

"Why do you say that?" he frowned.

Shit. She almost slipped up. "You bought a house behind my back so that's telling me you're leaving."

"Oh."

Just then a flood of water gushed between her legs. She opened her legs and a pool of bloody water settled on top of her towel.

"My water just broke!"

He flew off the bed to help her up.

"I have to wait until the contractions get closer," she said.

"Oh ok."

Jessica contacted Charmaine to tell her that her water had finally broken, she promised to let Trey contact her once she was en route to the hospital. She leaned against the headrest of her bed gently caressing her stomach subconsciously. She eased her butt up so that Trey could change the towel she sat on. He tossed it in thrash and tied the bag in a knot and washed his hands before returning to her side.

"Trey, I need to tell you something."

"What?"

"The baby...," an earth shattering contraction ricocheted across her uterus, she closed her eyes and gritted her teeth, her hand shot out and caught hold of his arm squeezing it tightly until the contraction subsided, "I'm sorry." She breathed. "That shit hurt."

Jessica grabbed her book and jotted down the time quickly.

"It's ok. I can handle it." Fifteen minutes later, she was curling her toes against the intense pain.

"I need some water," she said. Trey opened the water bottle on the side table and handed it to her. The pain was so unbearable she began to cry. Trey comforted her the best he could, he held her as a another contraction passed and she stiffened until the pain subsided.

"We need to go Jess." He helped her down the stairs and into the car.

Her purse and cell were already in her packed hospital bag. He rushed back to the house and pulled both bags out, locked the front door and tossed them into the trunk of the car. They pulled up to the hospital fifteen minutes later and he checked her in, within ten minutes she was wheeled to her private room.

The nurse brought her a gown to change into while another doctor inserted her IV line. Doctor Crichlow entered next and examined her, she was about ready to push. Jessica barely remembered everything that happened, she recalled her sisters and mother bursting into the room while the nurses scrambled around preparing for the delivery. Jessica felt an immense burning fire between her legs, her baby was crowing, five agonizing contractions later, Doctor Crichlow competently guided the baby out into the world. "Congratulations on your beautiful son, Jessica," her doctor beamed. Jessica got a small glimpse of him before they took him to the side to check his vitals. There was silence for a few seconds, then, she heard her son wailing loudly upon his entrance into the world.

Jessica was happy to hear her son's cries, her mother and sisters were crying while she wanted to pass out. Soon, the nurse brought the baby and rested him in her arms as another nurse cleaned her up. Jessica breast fed him for a quick minute before he was asleep. Her mother counted his ten fingers and toes, it was something she did to all of her Grands. His hair was jet black and curly, similar to hers, his skin was very pinkish and his ears were covered in fine dark hair which was strange to her, she'd never seen it on other babies, he looked so much like her too. As they rejoiced in the birth of the baby Trey sat outside of delivery room glaring at Ron.

Trey walked over to him aggressively, "What the fuck are you doing here?"

"The same reason you are here," he said harshly.

"You need to leave. Now!" he was enraged and was ready to kick Ron's ass for the hell of it.

"I have every right to be here!" Ron spat back.

"You have two seconds to turn around and leave,"

he balled his fists up, ready to knock Ron into next week.

Trey felt a hand on his back.

"Ron you need to leave, my family can't see you here?" Charmaine said.

"Why not?"

"Ron please! This is not the time or the place, you will have your answer soon."

He glowered at Trey. "She was mine first just remember that."

Trey snapped and he lunged at Ron, his hand missing Ron's neck by an inch.

"Trey don't!" Charmaine shouted as she blocked him from grabbing Ron. "He's not worth it."

"Watch your back, bitch," he sneered at Ron.

Mrs. Clarke and her daughters stepped out of the delivery room as Ron rounded the corner leaving, Trey straightened his shirt, trying to bring his pressure down.

"Trey, Jessica wants to see you."

"Thanks mum."

"What the hell was happening out here?" Olivia asked, "Why does he look so pissed?"

"Nerves I guess," Charmaine lied.

Trey watched Jessica as she cuddled her son, his anger melting right away, he walked over to her and kissed her. "He looks just like you," he chuckled.

"He's so sweet."

"Yes he is."

"You want to hold him."

"Nope, he's too tiny"

She snorted.

"How was it?"

"Those pains were hot as fuck. I'm not having sex for a year," she stressed.

"Yea right." They both laughed.

"Are you ok, you seem...off?"

"Nothing, I'm just happy you guys are ok. When are you getting out of here?"

"Not sure." Her baby was fast asleep nestled next to her breast.

"Can you put him in the cot for me, cradle his head and butt."

Trey held the baby and stared into his face. He looked exactly like his mother, there was nothing of him or Ron in his features. Mrs. Clarke peeked into the room. They were leaving, they wanted her and Trey to have time with the baby before visiting hours were over. Jessica promised to call when she was released from the hospital. Trey stayed with her for another hour before it was time to leave. He kissed her goodbye and she decided to take a nap before her son awoke for another feeding.

12

Both Jessica and her son were released from the hospital the next day and Trey collected them about 11:00 a.m. that morning. Mrs. Clarke and Charmaine were already at the house waiting for their arrival.

Trey carried the baby inside and placed the carrier in the couch, leaving his grandma to take over. He returned to the car and pulled the hospital bags from the trunk while Jessica and Charmaine settled in the couch next to Mrs. Clarke who held the baby lovingly in her arms.

"How was it?" Charmaine asked.

"Rough."

"It's rough now until you're pregnant again." Her mother chided.

"Nope. One and done," Jessica scoffed, "Sorry ladies, I'm gonna go lie down."

"I'll take him up and place him in the crib." Her mother left the living room and returned two minutes later.

"You really need to give him a name, I'm tired of saying the baby," said Charmaine.

"His name is Kareem Sommers," she said over her shoulder."

"I'm gonna stay with mummy for a while until I'm ready to go."

Jessica climbed the stairs gradually, her entire body felt sore and the huge sanitary napkin between her legs didn't help in making her feel comfortable. She looked in on Kareem before entering her bedroom. Trey was lying flat on the bed looking up at the ceiling. She crawled into bed and rested her head on his arm.

"You ok?" she asked him.

"Yea."

"Can you help mum with the baby if she comes to wake me, only wake me if he's hungry I guess."

"Gotcha."

The changes to their normal routine was exhausting, the late nights, lack of sleep and crying baby was no easy feat. Since Jessica was on maternity leave, she allowed Trey to sleep in as much as possible, plus, her mother was there to assist her with Kareem.

By the time Kareem had turned three weeks, Jessica had found a nice rhythm, her body was now in tune with his waking and sleeping patterns. She was feeling much better and she was able to step out and run any quick errands she needed to.

"Jess, you need to get more diapers, there are only a few left."

"Damn, I'll go get some now, I keep putting it off."

Jessica changed to leggings and a top; she chose a light coat to keep her body warm.

"I'll be back in fifteen minutes, I placed some milk in the fridge if he wakes before I get back."

Just as she pulled off, there was a knock on the door. Mrs. Clarke patted a cooing Kareem and looked through the peephole.

"Ron, what are you doing here? Jessica just left for the store, you can wait inside if you would like."

"Perfect. Thank you."

"Sure, come on in."

"What a beautiful boy," he said and took a seat in the living room.

"He's very handsome." Mrs. Clarke cooed at Kareem.

Ron began coughing violently, "Can I bother you for a glass of water?"

"Absolutely!" she rested Kareem into the baby swing set in the centre of the living room.

Ron coughed and inched closer to the baby swing. He brushed one finger across Kareem's soft cheek.

He slipped back to his seat as Mrs. Clarke's footsteps got closer.

"I am so sorry, but I have to run." He got up and sprinted towards the door.

"What about your water?" she called after him.

"Thank you," he said as he burst through the door.

She went over to the baby and tickled his tummy "That's strange isn't it Kareem?"

Ron sped off in his car, his head bobbing from side to side searching for any sight of Kareem's mother.

Jessica returned an hour later, "Sorry I took so long, there was a long line and then I ended up stopping by the office."

"It's fine, I fed him already and he went right back to sleep."

"I'm gonna shower before he wakes up."

"I cooked dinner early, get some while it's still hot."

"Ok." Jessica returned after her shower and took over from her mother.

21

"You should go get some rest, you've been on your feet all day."

"I am feeling tired indeed, I'll probably nap for 30 minutes or so."

Jessica plated herself some of the chicken and broccoli her mother had cooked, she sat in the living room and ate while watching tv, she looked down at her still protruding stomach, she couldn't wait to hit the gym. Kareem stirred but he didn't wake up so she settled back against the couch. Since she was on maternity leave she did not have to keep up with her files like before, she'd returned them to the office and delegated each file to her colleagues.

Around 3:00 p.m. Charmaine came over. "I need to talk to you about something, Jessica said."

Charmaine played with Kareem's chest and then sat next to Jessica.

"I need to get his DNA done asap."

"Has Ron been calling?"

"No. It's Trey. I can sense his angst, I know it's bothering him not knowing."

Charmaine did not know that her sister already knew Ron was Kareem's father.

"Do you know anyone that works at the lab?" She was dead serious.

"Jessica what are you asking me?"

"I need the results to show that Trey is Kareem's

father?"

Charmaine got up from her seat. "I'm not comfortable where this conversation is going, we could both go to jail. You can't manipulate those results, that's illegal."

"It's the chance I'm willing to take. You won't go to jail, I'll make sure of that."

"I'm not, I have two children," she shot back.

"Please Char, just give me the name and I'll handle the rest."

"Jessica you can't be serious, this is crazy."

"Wouldn't you do anything to save your family?"

"Yes, anything legal! What you're asking for is unethical and dangerous," she said angrily.

"This is my only choice," she barked.

"Trey will never forgive you if he finds out."

"He's never going to find out."

"I can't do this, you're playing with your child's life," she said anxiously.

"No, I'm trying to save my child's life."

"Trey needs to know the truth, are you losing your damn mind?"

"Just get me the fucking name and number, damn." She screamed.

Charmaine grabbed her purse and keys and headed out the door. She left her sister sitting there breathing hard. She was not about to lose everything she worked hard for because her sister fucked up her own life.

13

Ron came over five days later.

Jessica and her mother were in the baby's room chatting while she nursed Kareem. Trey was seated at the Island in the kitchen and he answered the door.

"Please I am not here to fight and I would rather we speak on the inside." Trey glowered at him for a few seconds before letting him by. Ron walked into the kitchen and Trey returned to his seat at the Island.

"Here." He slapped a folded sheet of paper onto the island in front of Trey. "This should explain everything."

Trey's pressure instantly shot up, "My man, why are

you here?"

Ron stepped back, "As I said, I am not here to fight, we both need to know the truth." It took Trey ten minutes to read the sheet of paper, at that instant Mrs. Clarke entered the kitchen and she was powerless to stop Trey. Trey attacked Ron, deliberately dealing him a brutal beating. Trey was incensed, he hammered Ron's face into a bloody pulp.

"Jessica!" her mother screamed.

She could hear a loud commotion downstairs, she quickly put the baby in the cradle and fixed her bra and top, she was flying down the stairs before she heard her mother screaming her name.

"What the hell was going on?" And as she turned towards the kitchen she could see Trey kneeling over Ron pounding his head into the floor. A small glimmer of joy rippled through her before reality set in that her husband was close to killing her ex.

"Trey, what the hell are you doing?" she squealed.

Trey got off of Ron, who was sputtering blood and probably broken teeth. He grabbed the sheet of paper from off of the Island and threw it at her. He then snatched his keys from the counter and headed outside, trailing bloody finger prints along the way. Jessica read the sheet of paper, she could no longer hear her crying mother nor did she hear the start of Trey's engine. What she read made her heart sink lower and lower and she instantly started to cry.

She stepped over to Ron, who was now sitting up, dabbing at his busted lip with the back of his hand.

"I had the right to know and so did he." Jessica smacked Ron hard across his face, she really walk to kick him in his balls but she knew her mother would intervene.

"You son of a bitch," she barked, Jessica lunged at Ron, raining hard blows all over his face and body. Her mother grabbed her shirt, yanking her backward. He had ruined her plans to get her husband back. What was she to do now?

"I am sorry Jessica, you left me no other choice."

Ron staggered to his feet and said, "I'll be back tomorrow to see my son."

Mrs. Clarke clutched her chest, as she watched the madness unfold before her eyes. Jessica looked at her mother, confusion and disappointment were etched all over her face. She was now obligated to tell her mother the complete truth. Jessica sat her mother down on the couch and begrudgingly told her the full ordeal of Kareem's conception.

"I'm just gonna start at the end, straight, no chaser," she sighed, wiping her weary eyes. "Trey is not Kareem's father. Ron is."

"Jessica!" her mother exploded, "How could you?" her mother's face contorted grotesquely.

Jessica wiped her tears away again.

"Is that why Trey nearly killed him?"

She nodded.

"This is downright distasteful?"

"Don't you love him? Weren't you guys getting along?"

"I do and yes."

Her mother began to cry.

"Mummy don't cry," seeing her mother so upset broke Jessica's heart even more, she was hurting everyone around her.

"You had no right in his home alone." Her mother's shoulders were shaking as she cried.

"I know mummy."

"Trey is a good man, you shouldn't have done that to him."

"I know," that's all she could say.

"Did you have any idea he was Kareem's father?"

"I don't have an answer for that," she said wiping more tears away.

"It's easier to fool people than convince them that they have been fooled," Mrs. Clarke said, she always remembered that great Mark twain quote. "I can't say that I'm not disappointed in you."

"Mummy?" she said. Kareem soon began to cry.

"Excuse me." Her mother no longer wanted to hear her excuses. She left the living room and went to check on the baby. Jessica stayed in the living room alone, lost in her thoughts. Trey was long gone, it made no sense to call him, he would never answer her calls. At 11:00 p.m. she went to bed. She switched on the baby monitor she had placed on top of the bedside table. Kareem's next feeding would be at 2:00 a.m.

When she awoke at exact 2:00 a.m., Trey was still not home, her mother ignored her when she stepped into the room so she fed the baby and returned to bed.

Jessica awoke at 5:00 a.m. and expressed milk and left it for the baby. Her mother didn't pay her any attention, and pretended to be fast asleep. Not in the mood for a verbal squabble with her mother she sauntered into the kitchen and made tea. While there she heard Trey unlock the door, he walked towards her in the kitchen. The temperature in the room dropped as they made eye contact, he hated her and she saw it in his eyes, without a word he turned and ran up the stairs. Jessica stayed in the kitchen, she was too afraid to face him, she wanted to comfort him but she dare not approach him. When he returned, he was dragging his two suitcases and his gym bag over his shoulder towards the door.

"Trey?" He turned and looked at her. "I am so sorry," she whispered.

They locked eyes. He didn't have to say it for her to understand their marriage was over, he was leaving for

29

good. He looked down before looking back up at her. There were tears in his eyes as well. He adjusted his gym bag and grabbed his suitcases by the handles. Jessica walked to the door and watched him pack his belongings in his trunk, he tossed the gym back in the back seat and sat in the driver's seat of his car and looked at her at the door.

He started his engine and pulled away. Jessica closed the door and instantly broke down, she cried out in anguish, she was bent at the waist with her face planted on the floor when she felt her mother's embrace, she held onto her mother's arms as wave after wave of heartbreak washed over her, she never wanted to lose Trey, but she had, she cried for the loss of her family, for the loss of her husband and for the loss of her friend, she didn't even get a chance to make it right.

Jessica did not know how long she remained on the floor, she did remember her mother helping her up the stairs and into her bed. She slept for a while until the baby needed to nurse. She was a zombie that entire day and her mother thought it best to keep a watchful eye over her.

"Jessica you need to eat baby." She stayed in bed for

two days, too beaten to eat.

"I'm not hungry mummy."

"Jessica, I know you are hurting, but you need to keep your strength up for your baby. I'm soon out of expressed milk."

Jessica rolled over. "Is he up?"

"I made you something hot to eat, see if you can eat a little bit." She took the bowl from her mother and swallowed a few hot spoonfuls of the food. Her mother kissed her on her cheek, "I'll be right back, let me check on Kareem."

There was a knock on her bedroom door as Charmaine walked in.

"Mummy called me."

Silence. Charmaine slid into the bed behind her sister, she wrapped her arms around her. Jessica intertwined her arms into her sister's arms. She sighed deeply and closed her eyes, just then Mrs. Clarke entered with baby Kareem, who was fussing in her arms. Mrs. Clarke laid him on the bed between Charmaine and his mother, "You have to snap out of this for him," Charmaine whispered into her ears.

"I just need one more day." She cried.

"That's fine. We are here for you sissy and I won't let you do this alone."

Jessica heard the loud roar of Ron's car as he pulled up outside, her mother went down the steps to answer the door. After seeing it was Ron she explained to him that he would need to come back the next day. He agreed. He had heard through the grapevine that Trey had left Jessica; after all he wasn't a pig like they thought.

"Is he gone?" Charmaine asked.

"Yes, but he'll be back first thing in the morning."

"Thanks," Jessica said.

Jessica kissed and played with a rooting Kareem, he cooed non-stop and kicked and jerked his tiny legs back and forth when she rubbed her face on his.

"I think he likes that," her mother said.

"He does, don't you baby," she sing-songed to Kareem.

"I'm going to help mummy with the washing etc," Charmaine said.

"Thanks hunny," Mrs. Clarke said to Charmaine.

Jessica spent the rest of the evening in her bed with her baby, the more time she spent with him the better she was feeling, she would miss Trey immensely but her mother was right, she had to get her shit together and pay attention to her son, he was her priority. She'd give Trey some time before she tried reaching out to him.

"I didn't tell you," she peeped behind her to see if their mother was in earshot, "Trey nearly beat Ron's ass when he showed up at the hospital when you were

32

giving birth, girl, Trey was enraged."

"I knew something was up when he came into the room, I could see he was upset but he didn't tell me anything."

"I had to beg Ron to leave."

"He's persistent if not anything else."

"Be careful with him, I know Trey is gone and it would be easy to slip back into 'something' with him.

"That's not where my mind is Char.

"I know, I'm just saying."

Charmaine stayed with Jessica just after the sun had set, once she was gone Jessica and her mother had a heart to heart, they ended the night hugged up together wiping tears from Jessica's eyes.

That Thursday Ron came over, he desperately wanted to see his son. Jessica greeted him at the door, she saw the swollen knot above his eye and the blue and black bruises around his cheek and chin, he grimaced as he flashed Jessica a huge grin... served his ass right. She guided him to couch and waited for her mother to bring the baby in, Mrs. Clarke placed Kareem in Ron's arms. Kareem was awake and cooing to his father. Ron was smiling from ear to ear as he nestled his son against him, he was excited to be holding his son, finally, "He looks just like you," he said to Jessica.

Ron was over the moon with his baby son, "What's

his name?"

"Kareem," She breathed, irritated. She couldn't keep his son away from him, but that didn't mean she had to enjoy it.

"Hello Kareem." Kareem had his tiny fingers tightly gripped around his father's index finger.

He looked up at Jessica, who was scowling at him.

"I'm sorry about Trey, I was in no way trying to ruin your relationship."

"Well since you want to go there, why show him first and not me?"

"You would have ignored me, just like you've ignored me all through your pregnancy."

Jessica didn't respond.

"All I want is to be a part of my son's life, that's it, as a matter of fact, this is for you." Ron handed her a cheque for three thousand dollars, denoted child support in the bottom left corner of the cheque.

"I don't need your money," she glowered.

"Jessica just take the fucking cheque, for fuck sake, this is about him, not you," he snapped.

"Whatever."

"Apologies, Mrs. Clarke, I didn't mean to curse in front of you."

Jessica looked at her mother and rolled her eyes.

From that day on, Ron spent an hour each day with Kareem, he was never late and soon felt comfortable enough to feed him without the prying eyes of his mother.

Jessica scheduled an appointment to meet with the Headmistress of the daycare she wanted Kareem to attend when she returned to work, she needed someplace easily accessible from her workplace. She filled out the application and decided to drop it when she was on the road running errands.

14

J essica returned home after her six week checkup to find Ron sitting with her mother in the living room with Kareem cradled in his arms, he was rocking Kareem to sleep. Seeing him always put her in a shitty mood.

"I know your Attorney has my parenting agreement."

"I haven't read it," he said, his attention focused on his son.

"I don't want you coming over here whenever you please."

"If it makes you feel better, I will read it and go from there."

"Thanks."

Since she received the all clear from her doctor that she could resume normal activities, she decided to hire a personal trainer to help her get back into shape. She went to her bedroom and switched into a jeans and t-shirt. She found Kareem drifting in and out of sleep, while Ron made bubbly noises with his mouth, he was the cutest thing when he flashed his toothless gums. He was developing so fast, she didn't want to miss anything, soon, she'd be back to work and he'd be in daycare. She didn't plan to do this without Trey but he was no longer a part of their world, now she was a single mother.

Trey had moved into his home on Carters, he stayed locked indoors for about two weeks, after he realized he was not mentally capable of working. The only visitor he allowed was Cameron, who brought his groceries and kept him up to date with the happenings of the outside world. For the past six weeks, his manager was running everything, he too was asked not to contact him outside of emergencies. Trey needed space and he needed time to think. He sat on his pool deck scrolling through photos of him and Jessica, he wondered whether she and Ron had rekindled their relationship now that they had a baby together. It didn't matter anymore, his Attorney had already drawn up the divorce papers, she would soon be a free woman to be with whomever she desired.

He missed her tremendously, he wondered if she missed him, she hadn't called or texted him in the weeks he was gone. He missed the smell of her hair; the softness of her body, her touch, he wished she was there with him. Damn! He had to stop thinking about her. Trey caressed his hardened shaft under his shorts, gliding his hand along its length, he leaned his head back against the couch as the familiar pleasure rippled through his stomach. His arm stiffened as his fingers tightened their grip around his bulging member, rapidly moving up and down, his hips bucked and thrashed rhythmically until he came, a long stream of cum squirted out onto his hand and down his fingers. He staggered to his bedroom and washed up, with nothing else to do, he grabbed a few more beers and took up his position on the couch.

Nine weeks to the day Trey had left, Jessica was served divorce papers. She thanked the process server and shut the door scanning the papers. Trey had really filed for divorce. She knew it was bound to happen but she still was not prepared at all. Her mother was still staying with her and her father was visiting for a week. Jessica also had to explain to him the situation with Ron, it seemed this would be her destiny...reliving her past time and time again.

"What is it?" he asked.

"Divorce papers."

"I'll leave you to it then." He returned to the baby's room with his wife.

"I'll be back soon." She called upstairs to her parents.

Jessica took the papers and tossed them into the passenger seat. An hour later, she was standing outside of Trey's home on Carters. It was a nicely designed home, with two huge mahogany doors, big windows, manicured lawns and a fairly decent sized garage, she could see the glistening pool water from the space between the wall and the fence. She walked back to the front and knocked on the door.

Trey opened the door, baffled to see Jessica standing there.

"Can I come in?" He stared at her momentarily before stepping aside.

"Sure."

Jessica entered and looked around, inside was even more immaculate than outside. His taste had surely improved from when she first had dinner in his home across the street. She was certain he had hired an interior designer to decorate this masterpiece.

"Your place is nice." It was designed similar to hers, the kitchen had the same marble countertop and island. And his living room faced the fireplace and onto a walkout patio.

He look disheveled and unkempt, he needed a haircut and his beard was bushy and wild. She sensed an air of animosity about him. She decided to give him a temperature check before she delved deeper.

"I got your papers."

She joined him on the couch, "All you have to do is sign."

She could see his temple pulsing. "Is it that easy for you to walk away?"

"I told you before that if Kareem was his..."

"I'm not signing these papers," she persisted.

"It makes no sense to prolong the inevitable."

"I love you Trey, I don't want to give up on us," her eyes misted.

He looked at her contemptuously, "Sometimes love isn't enough."

"I mean nothing to you?" she raised her hand to her chest as she waited for his reply. "Tell me what I need to do, to make this right?" she cried.

"You shouldn't have slept with Ron, let's start with that."

"You make it seem like I did that on purpose."

"Now only you would know that."

She watched him briefly, "I'm not giving up on us so easily. I'm not signing this."

"You share a baby with another man, where can we go on from there?"

"So what? I can share my life with you and Ron has nothing to do with us."

"Maybe you can make it work with him."

"Is that what you want?" she was incensed.

He glared at her. Within an instant, he was on top of her, ripping her panties off. He was deep inside of her in seconds. Jessica wrapped her legs around him, happily coaxing him to fuck her. He plunged into her savagely. The sweet pain of his long shaft ripping into her was maddening, she was soon groaning as her climax radiated from her wet centre down her legs, "turn around" he demanded, as she flipped over he slammed into her, sending shockwaves deep into her belly, Trey fucked her so hard, his knees rattled, Jessica felt hot tears rolling down her cheeks, she closed her eyes tight and grimaced against the pounding she was taking, digging her nails into the soft cottony couch, praying he would finish. He felt her walls contract around him steadily and he grunted loudly as cum splattered her insides. He slowly withdrew from her and instantly regretted what he'd done. He collapsed on the big couch, too exhausted to move. When their breathing had returned to normal, she rolled onto the floor and found her torn panties.

She watched him silently, "Cut your beard, you look like shit," she adjusted her clothing and made her way to her parked car. Trey pulled his boxers and jeans up, he chuckled at her comment, she was feisty and he loved that about her. He pulled his cell out and called his barber and scheduled an appointment with him for a home visit.

On her drive back home, she called her mother to let her know she was on her way home, she did not tell her she was going to see Trey. Kareem was fine, he was fed and asleep so she could relax and take her time on the road. Jessica was alarmed at Trey's appearance, she had never seen him looking so unkempt. She had no intention of sleeping with him, that wasn't why she went over to his home, but she had no regrets, it is what it is, at least he didn't hate her completely, she thought he would have found her reprehensible, but, maybe he just needed a nut and used her body to get off.

Her cell rang, it was her Attorney, she had received the signed parenting Agreement from Ron's Attorney and a copy would be sent to her in the mail. The Agreement stated that Jessica would remain Kareem's primary caregiver and visitation would arranged amicably between both parents, Ron was not permitted to drop by unannounced or increase his allotted time of two hours per visit with Kareem, the Agreement will be amended as Kareem grew older; at present Ron was not allowed to remove Kareem from his primary residence without Jessica's consent. She breathed a sigh of relief, she had Ron under control as it related to their son, hopefully, this arrangement would last.

Jessica's thoughts returned to Trey, hopefully, he was warming up to her and his little nut was proof he had forgiven her somewhat. She raised the volume on her radio and sang all the way back home. By the time she arrived, Kareem was still asleep, so she showered and ate dinner with her parents. As 8:00 p.m. rolled around, she was in her room, nursing Kareem and after he fed, she burped him and he slipped into a blissful sleep.

She was laying him on his side, when her cell rang, it was Ron, Jessica sucked her teeth before she answered.

"Yes Ron."

"Can you send me a photo of Kareem?"

"Now?"

"Yes, my kids would like to see their little brother." He was soft-spoken, almost too soft-spoken.

"Ok. I just put him down, so give me a minute."

"Ok. Thanks."

Jessica angled the phone camera in front of Kareem, she snapped two photos and sent them to Ron. She was trying to work with him because of Kareem. She racked that up to her good deed of the day.

That Saturday, Jessica got ready to meet her personal trainer, she was in pretty respectable shape for her lady who had a baby not too long ago. But, she wanted to get back to her pre-baby body. She kissed a robust Kareem and said goodbye to her mother before heading through the door. Jessica did not know how she got so out of shape, she was hardly able to keep up with her trainer, she struggled with each exercise, and routines that she killed at home were now kicking her ass in the gym. After an hour of weight lifting and cardio, she dragged her sore body to her car.

When she returned home, Ron was parked outside, she had forgotten she had told him it was ok for him to come over. He always stayed in the living room with Kareem, this time he was on the patio holding him securely in his arms.

"Hey big boy," she greeted Kareem, he smiled and kicked when he recognized his mother, he also kicked and smiled at his father to her annoyance. He had the prettiest smile she had seen on a baby. Ron noticed Jessica's work out attire, he loved everything that he was seeing, the tight spandex cupped and magnified her curvy figure. His rod twitched as his memory banks flooded with thoughts of a naked Jessica writhing beneath him.

"Ron?" she snapped her fingers in front of his face.

He positioned himself so that she would not see the sudden bulge in his pants.

"Sorry, what did you say?"

"Did you get the pics last night?"

"Yes, they are fascinated with having a sibling."

"They would be."

"Thank you, I really mean that," he said.

She smiled at him softly.

Kareem made a sucking noise and stuffed his finger in his mouth and began sucking harder, "I think he's hungry."

"I think you are right?" he laughed.

"Let me go shower and then I can feed him."

For that small moment, she wondered...the thought scared her...she quickly brushed it away, it must be her hormones, it had to be.

15

With Kareem now three months old, Jessica was back at work. Her mother had returned home and she felt completely alone and helpless, many nights she cried, cried when Kareem was crying and she didn't know how to comfort him, cried because she didn't have a partner to ease her burdens and cried because the universe was beating her at every turn. Jessica's days started at 4:00 a.m., she got up, made breakfast and got herself ready and then Kareem, thankfully, the nursery accepted him and they prepared his milk once she dropped him off.

She was in meetings constantly, a number of

accounts were reassigned to her which she needed to go through and make her necessary recommendations to push the accounts forward. During the day, she would call the nursery periodically to check up on Kareem, this day however, she was running late to collect him, she was forced to call Ron to collect him from the nursery.

"Can you take him home with you until I am finished?"

"Sure, no problem."

"I'll pick him up when I am done, thanks."

"Don't worry, just call me when you get in and I'll bring him over."

"Thanks. I'll call you later."

Jessica returned to the files and loose papers plastered across over her desk. As she scanned each sheet of paper, she amended her notes on the database. It took her an extra two hours to complete all of her paperwork; she rubbed her eyes and signed out of her work account. It was 8:30 p.m. Her boss, was also still at work, she said goodnight to him and headed to her car. As she pulled off, she called Ron to tell him she would soon be home.

Finally home, she stripped and showered and returned to the kitchen to make a cup of tea. She popped some leftover food into the microwave and sat at the Island until Ron and Kareem arrived.

Kareem was bundled into a sweater, cotton pants and socks and he was fast asleep. She took Kareem from Ron and placed him into the swinger, she removed his coat and checked him for bruises or anything unusual. She did it often, as demanded by her mother and now it was a force of habit. Ron placed his baby bag on the kitchen counter and joined her in the living room.

"I took him to see the kids earlier, they were ecstatic to see him, I hope that is ok," he said cautiously.

"I'd rather you ask me first," she said sharply.

He raised his hands in surrender. "I will from now on."

"How did Lydia feel about that?"

"Lydia and I are no longer together." He felt ashamed and he observed her closely.

"Sorry to hear that."

"Are you really?" he asked cautiously.

"You left me high and dry for Lydia, remember?"

"It was a difficult situation Jessica, I've told you that before."

A little cry came from Kareem, Jessica peeped at him but he didn't wake.

Ron cleared his throat, in all seriousness, "Why did you say I raped you."

"I never said you raped me." She looked at him shocked.

48

"Did you feel like I raped you?

"No. You were too rough and I did say no."

"Women say that shit to their man but it doesn't mean she doesn't really want sex and you like rough sex," he said amazed.

"Not that rough," she snorted.

"Interesting!"

They stared at each other awkwardly, the air was charged with desire, he leaned in to her but she shifted away at the last second.

"I think you should go." She avoided his glare.

"Are you afraid of what might happen or what you *want* to happen?"

"Got damn Ron, what is wrong with you?" she snapped.

"I would have never hurt you Jessica, I would gladly admit that I lost control that day." he said softly.

"I told you to stop."

"Yea but you were soaking wet, I didn't think that meant anything."

"Get out of my house." She was pissed.

Ron busted a ferocious laugh.

"Ok, I'm going. We are not done with this conversation, I have a right to defend myself and clear my name." He walked over to Kareem and kissed him on his forehead.

"Could you not kiss him in his face, I don't know

where your mouth has been?"

"I know where I'd like my mouth to be."

"OUT." She pushed him towards the door, he was laughing so hard, he couldn't speak.

She slammed the door shut as soon as his feet hit the ground outside.

"Oh Jess, come on, don't be so uptight, I'm kidding," she heard him say behind the closed door.

She returned to the living room and scooped Kareem from the swing, she carried him to her room, where she had already spread his blanket and laid him down, it was easier to have him in her bed when he got up for a feeding, she could feed him right there in her bed. Her cell chimed, it was a message from Ron stating that he was sorry and she needed to relax. She threw the phone to the bottom of the bed and nestled against Kareem,

Jessica was delaying sleep, so she switched the tv on. At 11:00 p.m. Kareem started to cry, she turned him onto his stomach so he could see her, as he smiled, a little dribble dripped onto his chin, he pushed up and down on his arms simultaneously kicking his feet while looking into her eyes. She played with his little chin until he started fussing again. Jessica cradled him across her thighs and she removed her breast to nurse him. Kareem nursed close to an hour and a half, when he was satisfied, she burped and cradled him in her arms.

She loved his baby smell, she kissed him repeatedly on his little fingers before placing him on his side.

She replayed the moment Ron tried to kiss her earlier in the evening, she was not about to kiss him, but, there was something there, she would blame it on her hormones, she never thought about Ron sexually after that day in his home, after all she hated him, but what the hell was she feeling for him.

She picked her cell up and dialed, he answered on the first ring.

"What are you doing?"

"Nothing, watching tv," he said.

"Wanna come over?"

"Jess, you're making this harder for both of us."

"I'm still your wife." She didn't want to be combative but he was acting like a stranger.

"How is Kareem?" He had never asked her about her baby after he left.

"He's asleep."

"Shouldn't his mother be asleep?"

"Yup she should...I miss you, don't you miss me?"

"I don't think that matters anymore."

"What does that mean?"

"Nothing."

Kareem soon starting crying again.

"Trey I have to go, Kareem is up."

"Cool."

She threw the phone to the side and picked up Kareem, she checked his pamper, he wasn't wet and he was full so she patted his back until he settled down and returned to sleep. Instead of bothering Trey again she stretched out comfortably under the covers and drifted off to sleep.

Her alarm sounded at 4:00 a.m., she crashed her palm into it, almost breaking the fragile alarm in two. She pushed the covers off, kissed Kareem good morning and stumbled to the kitchen. The lights were still on, she had drifted to sleep and totally forgot to turn them off.

She made a quick breakfast and dashed upstairs to shower and dress Kareem. When she finished getting herself ready she changed him into his outfit, took him downstairs and placed in his swinger while she ate. He was still asleep when she put him into his car seat. Eventually, he woke when she handed him to the daycare nanny and kissed him goodbye, she handed his baby bag to the assistant and scrambled back to her car.

She sighed as she drove into her parking spot. She had a few morning showings she needed to prepare for and then it was mainly deskwork for the remainder of the day. Her last showing finished around lunchtime and before she knew it she was heading to Trey's home, when she pulled up to his home she noticed a different vehicle parked outside, it was a brand new 4x4 truck neatly parked on the street, his license plate was attached to the front and back of the vehicle, she guessed he upgraded, she exited her car and walked to his door, she knocked and waited for him to open. When he did, she entered and he closed the door.

"What are you doing here?" his manner was cold and stern.

He looked so good, he had taken her advice and cut his hair and beard. He returned to the couch and inspected suspiciously. From Jessica's view she could see the outline of his flat stomach through his tight shirt. She walked boldly over to him and planted herself in front of him, she bent at the waist and arched her back seductively and rested both of her arms beside him in the couch, there was nowhere for him to run. She was face to face with him. S1he kissed him slowly before straddling him, she glided her hands down his chest and into his shorts.

Before she could go further, he grabbed her hands and stopped her.

"Jessica this isn't going to happen," his mouth was set in a thin line.

"Why not?" She was flabbergasted.

"'Cause that's what I said,"

She was shocked "You really don't want me anymore!" her comment was more of a statement than a question. She was stunned and wounded. She swung her legs back over him, stood and adjusted her dress. She stormed like a hurricane to his front door, slamming it against the house as she exited, she unlocked her car and rumbled through her bag for the brown envelope containing the divorce papers and a pen, she rushed back into his house and slapped the divorce papers onto his counter, she scribbled her signature on the dotted line and then turned towards him, she flung the bundle at his head. Trey ducked, avoiding the flying papers, she glowered at him, her chest rising and falling with each breath she took. Finally, she turned to the door and walked outside to her car.

16

S he started her engine and sped off, she wiped the streaming tears from her eyes. She couldn't put her emotions into words, his rejection crushed her more than she could describe. She guessed she was right, the last time they had sex was just a way for him to bust a nut. Jessica pulled into her parking space and shut off her engine. She sat there for at least ten minutes before she could muster up enough courage to fake smile all the way to her office. She closed her office door and took her phone off the hook.

Trey's rejection shook her to her core, to think about the way he treated her would mean she would end up crying and she couldn't be a crying mess at work, she didn't need any more office gossip about her. She would cry in the safety of her home. She forced herself to focus on work, she read and reread emails and still couldn't focus on what she was reading. She thought of Kareem of his smiling happy face, she would soon be able to hug him and kiss him.

"Jessica, these Mitchell hotel sales came in today and I need the updated portfolio soon," her boss said as he appeared at her door. "Are you ok?"

"Yea, just a lot on my mind," she tried to sound upbeat.

"So, you are good with that?"

"I'll have them done by Friday."

"Good, thanks."

The clock struck 4:00 p.m., and Jessica was already through the door. She collected Kareem from nursery and headed home. She set him in his swinger and set the device's mode to a light rotation to keep him occupied. She made a quick dinner, periodically checking on him as she cooked. It was Wednesday evening so she knew Ron would be over at some point to visit with his son.

She set her dinner and water on a tray and placed it on the coffee table. She ate and laughed while watching a comedy on the tv. The noise from the tv jumped Kareem from his sleep, he jerked his hands and feet back and forth while the pretty mobile rotated above him. Just as she was about to take him out, Ron parked at her curb, she heard his loud engine die when he shut it off.

She unlocked her door and returned to the couch. He brought over another child support payment and a basket full of toys and clothing for Kareem.

He went to the washroom and washed his hands before picking Kareem up and kissing him on his chest. At the sight of his father, Kareem shot him a huge gummy smile. Ron truly delighted in spending time with his son.

"Are you ok?"

"Yes." Her eyes remained glued on the tv.

Ron sat with Kareem on the patio, leaving Jessica in her funky mood. Kareem began to fuss and Ron brought him back to Jessica.

"He might need changing," he said.

"Did you check him?"

"No."

She pulled his pamper aside and said to Ron, "He needs changing, here, you take him." She handed Kareem back to Ron. Jessica took a small plastic baby changing mat and wipes from Kareem's baby bag and spread it open on the couch; Ron placed him on the mat which was between him and Jessica.

"I haven't done this in a long time."

He gingerly opened the snaps at the side of the pamper, as soon as he pulled the top of the pamper back, a shot of urine splashed directly onto his shirt.

Jessica chuckled, her soul was to beaten to laugh heartily, "I'm so sorry, I forgot to tell you to be careful."

"It's ok," he dabbed at his chest with a clean wipe.

"Hey little man, that wasn't cool baby." He held both of Kareem's legs together and lifted him gently to remove the used pamper and placed a clean dry one beneath him. He fastened the snaps and put his long pants on.

"See that wasn't so bad." Ron sat him up and rested him against his chest. He tried to touch Ron's beard as he cooed and sputtered in his own little language.

Jessica's telephone rang, she picked the phone up after the third ring and spoke to her mother briefly, she wanted to check on her and Kareem before she forgot and then it got too late for her to call. They ended the call after ten minutes and she returned to the couch next to Ron.

"Are you sure you are ok?"

"Yup."

"Is it true?"

"What?"

"It's over between you and Trey?"

She ran her hand behind her neck, "Yup, it's over."

Jessica wondered who was telling her business to Ron, he was somehow always a step ahead of her.

"I'm sorry, I mean that honestly."

"You should be this is your fault."

"If that's the way you feel, then yes, it is my fault."

"You had sex with me, a married woman and yet you came inside of me knowing all of that.

"Why do we have to always argue?"

"Because you make me sick Ron, you have ruined my life," she screamed.

"I didn't always make you sick." Her words cut him like razors across his bare flesh.

"I'm gonna go shower?" Kareem was asleep on Ron's shoulder and she needed to separate from him.

She stripped and turned the water on full blast, she washed her hair before lathering, she heard the door of the bathroom close and in stepped Ron. He was completely naked. The water soaked his lower abdomen first and then his chest. He closed the gap between them and stood inches from her.

"Don't." Her protest was weak and timid.

He leaned in and kissed her; her upper lips weren't thinking straight and neither were her lower lips, she accepted his kiss and after a slight hesitation, she also accepted his swollen shaft as he slowly eased inside of her. Jessica never compared her lovers but out of all of them, Ron was indeed the best, Shit! Her body was no longer her own as he drove her insane, he kissed her desperately, licking water from her round breasts. He lifted her and wrapped her thighs around him, he took advantage of her opened legs, the wider she spread them the deeper he penetrated her. She sunk her teeth into his shoulder as he pounded her out in the bathroom she once shared with her husband, her legs began to quiver as her climax came in strong waves, with each deep stroke, fireworks lit her hot slit afire, soon her whole body was burning, he expertly kneaded her ass as he devoured her womanhood, within seconds his thrusts quickened and his body jerked as hot cum blasted inside of her. A massive groan escaped Ron's lips as his cum pulsed and squirted into her.

He released her legs and she wobbled a bit, she felt awfully lightheaded. The piercing screams of Kareem echoed through the door. She washed her body off and dashed from the shower, she ignored Ron and flew through the door. She tossed on her robe and dashed into Kareem's room.

"What's wrong sweetheart?" she lifted Kareem from the cradle and took him back to her bedroom. She sat on her bed with him nestled in her arms, he angled his mouth towards her breast. He was hungry. She removed her breast and began to feed him. Ron toweled off in the bathroom and walked out completely naked, he started filing through his crumpled clothes in a heap on the floor searching for his boxers. Her eyes glazed over his impressive build and she averted her eyes when he caught her watching him. He dressed quietly and tossed the towel in the laundry basket.

"Do you need me to stay?"

"No, we are fine."

"Jessica..."

"I don't want to talk about it."

"Ok."

"Lock the door when you leave."

"Are you sure?"

"Yip." She couldn't even face him, she felt totally embarrassed.

He left her and a nursing Kareem in the bedroom, he locked the front door behind him and sat in his car, he was pissed with himself. Yes, he was very attracted to Jessica and she was the mother of his young son but she was still mourning the loss of her husband due to him. He finally started his engine and headed home. When he opened his door, the emptiness inside overwhelmed him, his home was empty; no woman, no kids, no laughter, there was no one to run into his arms when he came home. Hopefully, as Kareem got older, Jessica would allow him to stay over some nights. He walked into his den and sat scrolling through photos of his children. It brought him immense joy and he prayed that one day he would have a family with that perfect someone.

He thought of Lydia, their relationship did not work out sadly, after six months, she was still too full of resentment to give them a fair chance, he couldn't blame her, she had tried. His relationship with his kids did get better, they called him often and he would take them out on weekends, he loved spending time with them. He mixed himself a strong drink and downed it in one gulp. Would Jessica ever come back to him? Would she even want him after all the shit he had done to her? He was grateful that she trusted him enough to collect Kareem and keep him when she was running late from work; he was able to spend even more time with his son. He would gladly take her back but he would leave that decision to her, he would make her happy, she and Kareem would be well taken care of, he was sure of that.

The following evening, he was in her bed again. She went to bed for a nap while he played with Kareem downstairs. When he was ready to go, she told him he could rest him on the blanket next to her. He sat next to her after he had laid Kareem down, he was naked.

Jessica was a beautiful woman, his need to feel her again drowned out any logical thought. He shouldn't have touched her but he did; he shouldn't have kissed her but he did. He nimbly walked his fingers beneath her shirt and caressed the soft flesh of her breasts, she instantly woke up and looked at him, she saw that he was naked and very aroused. He stood and kneeled on the bed, she didn't' stop him when he hiked her dress up and removed her panties. She stopped breathing when he moved over her and licked her neck and breasts. Her fingers found her enlarged clit, it blossomed in anticipation of his thickness penetrating her, she spread her legs wide allowing him to sink every inch of him between her silky flesh and further inside of her. He shivered as his bulging erection consumed every space of her centre, the fragrant smell of her sweet nectar intoxicating him, his hips were moving at the speed of light as he slammed into her repeatedly, "I can never give you up," he said, his breath catching in his throat but somehow in tune with his thrusts.

An airy whisper was her only response as her slippery centre convulsed and her milk seeped from her breasts, Jessica was soon aware of an odd feeling on her right breast, Kareem was suckling on her drizzling milk, but she was in the midst of an exquisite climax. Ron eased off of her after seeing Kareem hungrily drinking from his mother and he ended his climax off of the bed and out of Kareem's sight. Jessica on other hand was coming, uncontrollably, she was powerless to stop Kareem or herself as the surge of her climax rattled her. To Kareem's annoyance, Ron removed him from nursing and he instantly began to cry. Once her climax sated, she breathed deeply and shakily got off of the bed. She wobbled into the shower and rinsed her body quickly before returning to nurse Kareem.

Ron all about passed out on the bed and Jessica's arms barely felt able to support Kareem. As soon as he went back to sleep, she removed her breast and laid him into his cradle for the remainder of the night. When she came back they both doubled over laughing.

"I hope that's not a memory that would stay with him," she said embarrassed.

"Nah, he's still too young."

"I don't know what we are doing."

"Neither do I," he confessed.

"Maybe it's your way of getting over Trey."

"I shouldn't be doing this."

"I hear you."

"This doesn't mean anything. I...We...it won't work."

"I'm willing to try if you are."

"Ughhhh this is so fucked up." Maybe she was trying to get over Trey, but got dammit it should never be with Ron.

They sat and chatted awkwardly until it was time for him to go. Jessica walked him to the door and settled back into bed and was asleep before Ron had even turned the corner.

17

Jessica rose early and packed Kareem's bag with another set of clothing and refilled his wipe container. Kareem was also up, sucking on his thumb while his mother flitted around his room. She took him to the kitchen with her while she cooked three eggs and made coffee. She turned on his mobile and placed him back in his cradle while she showered and dressed; she then wiped him off and dressed him for daycare. She nursed him for fifteen minutes, grabbed her purse, workbag and Kareem's bag.

She tossed the bags in the trunk and then secured Kareem in his car seat. She checked her mirrors before pulling off and at daycare she handed Kareem off to his 'auntie' and drove to work. She dropped her bags in the chair in front of her desk and opened her laptop, she had promised to email her boss the updated Mitchell portfolio that Friday.

Jessica buried herself into her work, her soul was destroyed; she had been rejected by her husband and she had slept with a man she despised. She glimpsed at the photo of Kareem at the corner of her desk, seeing him made always her feel better, at least she was a good mother. She made her final edits and emailed the completed portfolio to her boss. She breathed a sigh of relief.

Her cell rang, just as she was heading to reception, the caller spoke before she did.

"Jessica, Jessica, how are you?"

"Good Morning!" she was cautious, she didn't recognize the voice.

"Jess, it's me, Timothy!"

"Oh hey, what's up?"

"I'm having a party at my house and I wanted to invite you."

"Uhhhh I'm not sure if..."

"Oh come on, it's a simple party."

"When is it?"

"Next Saturday."

"I might be free, send me the location."

"Great, I'm looking forward to seeing you."

She placed the cell down and went to find Syl. When she pulled her email up again, there was an email from Sara, her Attorney, she had sent her a copy of her Divorce Decree. Jessica was now a divorcee. She opened the document and read it bit by bit, when she felt the tears brimming, she closed the document and wiped her eyes, her divorce from Trey was not contentious, mainly because she refused any type of alimony from him which made the process much easier. She hadn't seen him since the day at his home, she spoke to him through Sara. They really had nothing to talk about anymore.

Jessica prepared for a showing at 10:00 a.m. She gathered her folder and papers and headed to her car. Within an two hours, she was back in the office. She opened her laptop and updated her records for the showing she had just completed. She swished around in her chair. Tomorrow, Saturday, she had an appointment with her personal trainer for an at home workout, she was tempted to cancel it, but she was seeing marked improvement in the way she looked, her stomach was much flatter than before Kareem, she was practically back to her pre-baby size and better.

She ordered lunch, a salad and fish plate which she dived into as soon as it arrived. She spent the balance of the day updating her database and fielding calls from a few irate clients. Jessica kept her eyes on the clock as the evening dragged on. By the time the clock struck four, she was over work. She hastily made it over to Kareem's daycare and collected him. Kareem was such a happy baby, he suckled on his finger and kicked his chubby legs out as he watched and listened to the sounds of the passing traffic. He was alert, and listened to her when she spoke to him and always smiled.

Jessica parked at her curb and grabbed all of their bags and with Kareem hooked on one hip, she dropped the bags at the door and fished around in her pocket for the key. She kicked the door open and then tossed the bags into the hall. She placed Kareem on his stomach in the living room where he could play a little with the soft toys she left for him. She flung her skirt and top over the top of the couch and joined him on the floor. She wiped him off and changed him out of his clothes from the daycare while he gurgled and dribbled, while she loved all over him, he soon started fussing so she cuddled him in her arms. She coed to him and he angled his mouth to her breast, she grabbed a wipe and cleaned her nipple off before allowing him to feed.

Jessica sat on the floor for thirty minutes, with Kareem latched onto her breast, once he was asleep, she placed him in his swing, while she prepared dinner. She eased him from his baby swing and laid him in her bed and formed a fortress around him with her pillows while she showered. She returned to the kitchen after her shower and finished her dinner.

By 8:00 p.m., she was in bed cuddled next to Kareem, who was still asleep. Jessica watched tv for a while until she fell asleep. At 11:00 p.m., he was nursing again and as soon as he finished, Jessica herself was also asleep.

Jessica's trainer arrived just before 9:00 a.m., luckily Kareem was asleep while they worked out on the patio. Within the hour, she was panting and sweating as Jeanette, her trainer, put her through a grueling forty-five minute workout, when they were finished Jessica stretched out on the floor of the patio exhausted, she paid her trainer her fee and walked her to the door, she returned to the living room and sat on the floor. Since Kareem was asleep, she flew up to her shower and washed off before he woke.

She peeked at Kareem in his baby swing and grabbed her protein shake from the refridgerator, she rolled up her workout mat and tucked it in a corner in her office, she then sat at her desk and swiped the dust with her hand, and eagerly watched the dust particles dancing up into the air. Trey had cleaned it out nicely, all of the baby boxes were removed, returning it back to its original state, she brushed a sheen of dust from a photograph of their wedding day. She took the photo up and traced one finger over Trey's smiling face, she quickly returned it to the desk and exited the office, it was too painful to think about him.

The loud roar of an engine alerted Jessica that Ron had pulled up outside, she made a quick glance in Kareem's direction, he was still knocked out. She unlocked the door and sat next to the swing, she switched the tv on and lowered the volume to barely audible when Ron entered and walked directly to Kareem. He kissed him on his chest and sat on the couch.

"How long has he been out?"

"Long."

"I forgot how much they sleep when they are babies."

"She swiveled her body to face him. "About last night, that shouldn't have happened."

"Yea, you're right, I'm sorry," he said delicately.

Jessica was taken aback. That was not the response she had expected. Ron was often crude and annoying to her.

"Good." She was hesitant to continue sitting in the same space as him, she felt edgy and pensive.

There was a loud knock at the door. Jessica peeped out and saw her sister standing there. She opened the door and Charmaine stepped inside. She greeted Ron in the living room, she wasn't expecting to see him there so early and she looked at her sister suspiciously.

She barely acknowledged Ron, she peeked at Kareem and sat on the opposite couch.

Charmaine picked up on the weird energy passing between Jessica and Ron. Jessica was too calm, a far cry from the venomous and lethal tongue she always had for him. Something was off...They avoided eye contact and Ron was way too fidgety. Charmaine grabbed her sister by her arm and dragged her to the kitchen.

"What's going on?" she whispered.

"Like what?"

Charmaine stared into her sister's brown eyes, she knew she was on some bullshit.

"What?" Jessica bristled.

"Nothing, I hope you know what you are doing sissy."

At that moment, Kareem began to cry, Ron immediately took him from the swing and comforted him and he settled down. Charmaine released her sister's arm and walked back to the living room and sat next to Ron, she loved cooing to her nephew. His bright eyes darted between her and his father, their moving lips fascinated him into a big bright smile.

"Char, a minute," she took her onto the patio, "Can you watch Kareem for me on Saturday?"

"What's happening Saturday?"

"Timothy asked me to go to some party of his."

"Who is Timothy?"

"Timothy from school!"

"Where'd he come from all of a sudden?" She asked eyebrows raised.

"Anyway, can you watch him?"

"Sure."

"It's at 8:00 p.m., so you might have to keep him overnight," she pleaded.

"That's fine, just make sure you pack all of his supplies." She insisted.

"Thanks."

18

A loud wail, jumped Jessica from her sleep, she sighed and listened as Kareem cried even louder. At six months old, he hated sleeping in his cradle, he always wanted to sleep in her bed and many nights, whenever he woke and realized he was not in her bed, the cries began, she found him peeping through the cradle bawling his eyes out, once she brought him to her bed, he'd nurse and eventually go back to sleep.

The next morning, she found him asleep under her arm, since he was more active, she had to have a camera installed in his room to make it easier to view him at night. Since Kareem was born, she cleaned even more than before, between her family and Ron, someone was always in her home, plus, Kareem was crawling and trying to stand so she was forced to clean and keep her home as sanitary as possible.

Jessica depended heavily on Ron and Charmaine, they both were constantly assisting her with whatever she needed especially when it came to Kareem and as soon as Charmaine came into her home she ambushed her.

"I need you to watch Kareem again," she said smiling.

"Timothy?"

Jessica went on numerous dates with Timothy, they went on dinner dates, they went to parties, movies, the beach, you name it, Jessica and Timothy were attendance. For the most part, they were friends and he never crossed the line and she was happy with that. She liked him but she wasn't looking for anything serious and he was fun to hang out with him, she deserved a little happiness after all. That Friday night, Timothy picked her up around 7:00 p.m., they were going to a moonlight picnic with other school mates. To her delight, she saw Charlie there and chilled with him a little. Jessica couldn't remember the last time she had such strong alcohol and the four shots she drank made her feel thrilled and excited.

The moonlight picnic was still going at 4:00 a.m. in

the morning. She was cold and since they were no buildings to huddle in, she and timothy sat in the car gossiping about their former classmates. They could see the outline of the others on the beach from the moonlight and the loud bass of the music kept thumping through the car doors. He took her hand in his and faced her; they stared at each other for a long moment.

"What?" she immediately felt shy and silly.

"Nothing."

He took her face in his hands and they shared an intense steamy kiss, his lips were soft and supple and she was soon lost and shamelessly caught herself moaning into his mouth. His cologne was magnetic and she couldn't resist him. Blind lust was driving her and all she wanted was to feel him inside of her. They parted briefly to remove the necessary items of clothing and after he rocked his seat back and she sat over him. He quickly pulled open his armrest and pulled out a condom and she continued kissing him as he broke the condom rapper and slipped it over his thick six inches.

Jessica slid down on him, it wasn't what she was accustomed to but she wasn't going to complain. He reached up to take her mouth again.

He stopped, "Let's go in the back seat." She climbed into the back seat and laid on her back and he followed next, she angled his head between her legs and spread her legs wider as he savored her delicious juices, she arched her back and squeezed her breasts. She felt his tongue lapping at her tender clit as she rolled and gyrated her hips against his warm tongue. Jessica hissed as he spent copious amounts of time teasing and exploring her hot slit, she squeezed her legs around his head as the nerves between her legs exploded driving her to an exhilarating climax. He watched her eagerly from the view between her legs, he loved the way she reacted to his flickering tongue. His dick was hard as a rock and he couldn't wait. She guided him above her and he excitedly slid inside of her, but, he wanted to savor this experience, there was no rush, just slow and easy. They stayed glued together, both enjoying the sensual flow of his measured strokes. His mouth met hers, kissing her purposefully and gently, he rolled her nipple between his thumb and index finger, "Gosh Jess," she could feel his warm breath on her neck as his strokes grew needier and more urgent. Jessica wondered if they were making love, she'd never been made love too, this was different, this was satisfying. The slow massage of her walls coaxed her to another trembling climax, the base of the music drowning out her cries as she came loudly against Timothy's ear. The wet squishy sounds of her slit beckoned him to his own release, he pumped harder and faster until he regrettably blasted his seed.

He gently rested on top of her and her walls contracted around his throbbing shaft at will before he eased out of her.

Timothy carefully removed the condom and wrapped it in tissue. He sat back against the seat and pulled her legs up over him.

"I've never experienced anything like that before." She said.

Jessica might have been a single mother and divorcee, but she was a very hot commodity, he knew Jessica had no intention of being in a serious relationship with him and he was desperately hoping that she wouldn't end it too soon. "Are you this quiet during sex?" he asked astonished.

"No, I didn't know what to say." They both broke into boisterous laughter. Jessica was not a prude but she couldn't think of thing to say, she could talk her shit during the act but this time was different.

That moment ignited the sexual relationship between her and Timothy. He was the first man she brought to her bed after Trey, on the odd occasion, he would stay over until morning but for the most part he would leave her in the wee hours of the morning.

Timothy was not her type, of course, he was tall and lanky with little to no muscle mass, he was much fairer than Ron and his face was clean and free of any hair similar to a prepubescent boy. Jessica preferred her men buff and plus, he always looked as though he was squinting against a bright light. However, she did enjoy his company, he was hilarious and he liked making her laugh. He was a gentleman whenever they were together.

Jessica had told Charmaine about her 'situationship' with Timothy. She was wasn't thrilled when she heard about him but at least she was no longer brooding over Trey, her way of getting over him was shrouded in immaturity, but, Jessica was grown and had to take responsibility for her actions, She however, despised the thought that Jessica might be sleeping with Ron. Charmaine had a sneaky suspicion that they were having sex, she wasn't pleased with that idea either but she knew Jessica was head over heels in love with Ron before he left her for his wife and with Trey now out of the picture, she was easy prey.

Her suspicions were confirmed when she showed up at her sister's unexpectedly. It took Jessica noticeably longer than normal to open her door and using her spare key, she unlocked the door and stepped inside. What she heard, shocked her, Jessica was having sex with someone, the sounds of passionate wild sex escaped from her bedroom and down the stairs. Charmaine decided to sit at the kitchen island and wait but the primal sounds echoing down the steps made her quite uncomfortable and she switched from the kitchen to the couch. Finally!, Damn, she could hear chatter and shuffling feet as Jessica and her lover descended the stairs. She saw Ron first and then Jessica when she stepped around him, they both froze when they saw Charmaine. Ron stuttered something to Jessica and made a bee-line for the door.

Charmaine cut her eyes at her sister. Jessica grabbed a water and followed her into the living room and sat on the opposite couch, her hair was wild and she looked exactly like what had just been done to her... fucked!

"So you're fucking two men at the same time?" she barked.

Jessica rolled her eyes, "Quit with the self-righteous act, Char. I can't do this with you right now," she was in no mood to get into a screaming match with her sister.

"Why not, Jessica?"

"You're having sex with two different men and you're bringing all that shit around your son."

"I'm not bringing shit around Kareem." She shouted.

"You should be ashamed of yourself, fucking Ron? Are you crazy?" she said angrily.

"I can fuck whoever I want too and you need to mind your own fucking business." she screamed.

"Mind my business," she asked incredulously, "You bring all your business to ME,"

Just then Kareem awoke crying, their loud exchange jolting him from his sleep.

"I didn't ask you for any thoughts about what I'm doing with what's between my own fucking legs." Jessica snarled.

"Fine, I won't, her tone fragile and soft. You're playing a very dangerous game sissy, you've already been bitten in the ass once." Charmaine picked her up her bag, flinging the spare key across the kitchen counter and left.

Jessica ran up the steps and picked Kareem up, she placed him over her shoulder and patted his back gently, she squeezed his pamper to see if he needed changing, he soon quieted down and she returned him to his cradle. She crashed into her bed, she was pissed at Charmaine for breaking into her home and insulting and demeaning her. She walked into the kitchen, the sight of the key stalled her, and she gently played with the spare key on the counter. She rubbed her eyes, frustration building with each passing second. She found an almost empty bottle of wine, and poured out the contents into a big wine glass.

She was a single woman, she didn't need Charmaine's permission to entertain any man she chose, it was her right and her business, she didn't interfere in her marriage. She emptied her glass and placed it on the coffee table. If she had taken the time to listen to her, she would know that Jessica had no intention of rekindling anything with Ron, it was just sex, at least for her. It was true, she didn't completely hate him anymore but that didn't mean she wanted a relationship with him, she loved Trey and she would happily welcome him back if he came to her right that second.

What gave her the right, to judge her, she may need to rethink confiding in her sister. Jessica took the wine glass and placed it in the sink, she turned her lights off and crawled into her bed, she looked at the camera in Kareem's room and he was still fast asleep, she fluffed her pillows and settled in for some sleep. As soon as she drifted off to sleep, Kareem's cries wafted through the baby monitor, she reluctantly threw the covers off and entered his room, Kareem was teething and it made him cranky and unable to sleep. She changed her sheets as best she could with one hand and placed him on a clean blanket. She turned on her tv and kept the volume low while he nursed until he fell asleep on her breast.

Jessica hardly slept after that, Kareem was in and out of sleep the entire night, she needed to get him something for his gums so after breakfast she buckled him into his seat and headed to the pharmacy, while en route she called Charlie to see if the was on duty at work, he offered to pull her some soothing solutions by the time she arrived. Since it was a Sunday, the parking lot was pretty light enabling her to park closer to the entrance.

"Hey Charlie," he was at the front counter today.

"Hey Jess, hey big man," Kareem was bent at the waist, tapping on the counter. The lights from the ceiling above, casted a bright pretty circle on the counter and he was captivated by it. Jessica kept adjusting Kareem on her hip as he played with the spot on the counter. As she was discussing the teething medication, Timothy walked up to her.

"Jessica! Hey, I haven't heard you in a few days."

"Sorry, I've been busy, busy."

"What are you doing later?"

A lady stepped next to him, directly under him.

"Hello," she said. Timothy looked at Jessica shyly.

"Hello." Jessica said to her. An awkward silence ensued.

"Uh, Jessica," he said, "This is Sydney...my fiancé," he finished.

"Fiancé? Hmm...Congratulations," she said to Sydney. Sydney was a pretty young lady, very bubby and doe-eyed. Her long black hair hung delicately behind her small shoulders and she kept tossing it behind her head dramatically. They could easily pass for brother and sister or from the same family tree.

She hooked her hands into his, "Thank you."

82

"Oh my gosh, excuse me, I forgot to purchase something else I needed. It was nice to meet you Jessica."

"Same here," she said smiling. Turning to Timothy, she said, "Fiancé? Congrats," she was fuming.

"Jess I can explain later."

"Explain this, were you fucking me first and then her or was it vice versa?" She turned to Charlie, handed him a twenty and brushed past Timothy. Charlie's mouth was wide open as he took the cash and rung it in. He didn't even bother to call after her for her change, she was already out the door.

Jessica flew back home, she removed Kareem from his seat and he instantly began to cry, her energy was off and he sensed it. She blew hot heat through her lips. She placed him in his baby swing and walked to the kitchen and washed her hands. She removed a still agitated Kareem from his swing and placed him on his play mat on the floor and laid next to him. She teased and tickled his jiggly tummy to his delight. Jessica smelt an offensive odour coming from his pamper, she pulled it back a tad and held her nose. She turned him over and grabbed a few wipes and a new pamper she kept in the bottom of the swing. After she was done, she reclasp his onesie and they resumed their playful session. Within thirty minutes, he was asleep, she lifted him and took him to his cradle and returned to the kitchen.

Her cell started ringing, it was Timothy, she rejected the call and blocked his number. She turned it off completely and tossed it on the couch. She prepared lunch and ate it in the living room while she searched the tv guide for some relaxing tv. Jessica understood that she had some hard decisions to make, she was a one woman man. Thankfully, she was on birth control and she and Timothy always used protection, sadly she couldn't say the same for Ron. "Uhhhhhh," she screamed.

19

On Monday, when Jessica strolled into the office, Syl handed her five message slips, "This guy keeps calling you," Jessica glanced at the messages from Timothy, "He said its urgent and to please call."

"If he calls again, tell him I no longer work here." Jessica replied unbothered.

"Yes ma'am." Syl chuckled.

Jessica immediately set her bags down and opened her laptop, she always poured herself into her work, when she felt overwhelmed with life, it was her great escape from her reality. Her day was easy, there were no angry clients and no rush showings, she was able to take her time and get her work done, she updated her database and she actually was able to sit and enjoy her lunch.

Jessica left work at the end of the day and collected Kareem from nursery, she felt tired and miserable, she tried to keep her mood upbeat in order not to affect Kareem again and soon after she changed Kareem, someone was knocking at her door. She placed him on her hip and peeped out, her mother and Charmaine were standing there. She opened her door, stunned.

"Mummy, what are you doing here?"

"Hello baby, I came to spend a few days with you and Kareem," she said bashfully.

Jessica closed the door as they all filed into the living room.

"Let me see my grandson," she said sweetly. Jessica handed Kareem to her mother. Charmaine stood back watching the scene unfold.

"Mummy, Kareem goes to daycare now."

"I am aware of that, I missed him terribly so I came to spend some time with you guys."

Jessica knew her sister was responsible for this sudden appearance of their mother. "What about daddy?"

"He'll be fine, he's a grown man, he knows how to take care of himself," she looked at her daughter directly.

"Mummy I'm gonna put your things in Kareem's room." Jessica glared at her sister across the room; she subtly flipped her the bird, Charmaine smiled smugly before heading upstairs. When Charmaine finally left her mother sat her down to chat.

"What have you been up to?"

"Kareem....Work..., that's about it."

"Mummy why are you really here, did Charmaine put you up to this?"

"I wanted to come spend time with you guys," she answered, her voice smooth as silk.

"Since you're here, Ron has visitation with Kareem tomorrow."

"Fine."

"Well, mummy, I'll leave you to it then. She gleefully ran up to her room and slunk into her big bed. She switched on the tv and stretched out in the bed. Jessica did not know what to do with her time alone, her mother was with Kareem and she was free for the moment. She thought of Trey, she hadn't seen him over the last few months, she wondered if he was seeing anyone, a caring man like that didn't stay single for long. She punched his number into her cell, she thought long and hard before she swiped the green icon to initiate the call, she cancelled it, her anxiety was skyrocketing. He'd made his decision, it was best to leave him alone.

Mrs. Clarke strolled into Jessica's room, when Kareem started to fuss.

"I think he's hungry."

Jessica unclipped her bra and nursed Kareem, he had an odd habit of feeling her other breast while he fed. He'd also stare into her eyes and if she was speaking to him, he'd stop and listen before he continued to nurse. He fed for about an hour again before he finally fell asleep. Her mother placed him in his cradle and spent a little time with Jessica before she too fell asleep while her mother was speaking to her.

Her alarm sounded at 4:00 a.m., but she didn't need to do anything, her mother already had breakfast prepared.

"This French toast is delicious," she said to her mother.

"You are welcome." Her mother brought her a cup of coffee.

"I can get used to this mummy." she gushed.

"You seem to be doing just fine," she said very proud.

"Thanks, I need to go get ready though."

"Can you take care of Kareem for me?"

"Sure baby."

Jessica stripped naked and jumped into the shower, hopefully her good luck would continue throughout the day. By 6:00 a.m., she and Kareem were bustling through the door to her car. She dropped Kareem off to the daycare and sped into her reserved parking spot.

"Jess, the man wants to see you," Syl said.

"Fuck, what now?"

"Beats me hun."

Jessica dropped her bags on the office floor and went to see her boss.

He was on the phone and signaled for her to come in. She sat in the chair opposite him.

He hung up from his call and turned to her, "What's up with the Sylvan property?"

The Sylvan property was a huge 3 acre lot, rumours had it that the property was used as a mass grave site in the early 1900s.

"I'm hearing that big investors are afraid to touch it due to its history."

"Did you research it?"

"There's nothing concrete that I've found."

"No one wants to touch it with a ten foot pole," he tapped his pen against his desk.

"See if you can co-broke, we need to get that piece of shit sold."

"Cool."

"Thanks Jessica."

Jessica supervised three more interns throughout the day and by the time she got back to the office, it was time to collect Kareem. Traffic was always a bitch on a Friday and she just wanted to get home. She pulled up to her home close to 6:00 p.m. Her mother came out and lifted Kareem from his seat, Jessica was indeed greatful for the unsolicited visit. She heaved their bags inside and flitted around the kitchen searching for food.

Just after she arrived home, Charmaine came over and they all gathered around the kitchen island. Charmaine made small talk with their mother completely ignoring Jessica which infuriated her immensely.

"What is your problem with me?" Jessica finally asked, her tone sharp and angry.

"Well since you asked, I'mma tell you." Charmaine snapped. "You need to get your shit together."

"I told you before to mind your own business."

"And stop walking around acting like a got damn whore." She barked.

"Charmaine!" Mrs. Clarke yelled, horrified at what she had said to her sister.

"I'mma whore now?" Jessica shook her head in disbelief.

"Yes, tell your mother what you were doing in the bed next to your son with Ron," she turned to their mother, "Did she tell you she was sleeping with Ron again?"

"You are such a bitch." Jessica blurted out, she was

obviously hurt by her sister's comments.

"Stop it," their mother screamed. "This is ridiculous," Mrs. Clarke screamed at the top of her lungs.

Jessica left the kitchen and slammed her bedroom door shut.

"Charmaine you should not have spoken to your sister like that."

"Why not, I'm tired of coddling her grown ass." She was still angry and not about to apologize for how she felt. "I'm out," she kissed her mother on her forehead and grabbed her purse and walked outside to her car.

Kareem was still awake and Mrs. Clarke spent the balance of the evening entertaining him while Jessica stayed locked away in her room. Mrs. Clarke knew the sound of Ron's loud engine and she unlocked the door for him, he was there to visit with Kareem. When Jessica came down from the bedroom, she said hello to Ron and grabbed her protein shake from the refridgerator, she was still in fit mode. Her mother handed Kareem over to his father and he took him out on the patio, something was up and he wanted no parts of it.

Mrs. Clarke took the opportunity to chat with her daughter, she didn't like the news she was receiving from Charmaine, especially after the fight they had earlier. She knocked on the bedroom door and waited to enter. Jessica was on the bed watching tv, "Hey baby, can I speak with you for a moment."

"Nope." She was not in the mood for a serious pow wow with her mother, especially not about the men in her life.

She disregarded Jessica's answer and continued despite her attitude, she sat on the edge of the bed and faced her daughter, "I know that Trey leaving you was a hard pill to swallow, but, you won't find what you're looking for by spreading your legs to several men. Jessica's eyes widened in surprise, her mother's words stung painfully.

"Oh wow!" she felt wounded. "With all due respect mummy, this is not a conversation I want to have with you and correction I'm not sleeping with several men."

"Three men if you want to be specific, I am not judging sweet heart, I pray that you will open your eyes and see that this behavior is ungodly."

"Mummy stop." She removed herself from her mother's presence before the wrong words escaped her lips. She sat on floor of her bathroom crying. Twenty minutes later she heard a soft rap on the door.

"Jess open up."

She strained her hand up and turned the lock, Ron entered and sat opposite her on the bathroom floor.

Her eyes were red from crying, "Your mother isn't trying to bash you, you know that." He really wanted to ask her who else she was sleeping with but now wasn't the time. She eyed him curiously, "I could hear your conversation from downstairs."

"Come here," he patted the space on the floor next to him. Instead, she stretched out next to the tub staring at the ceiling, the warm heat from the tiles penetrating her back through her light shirt.

"Why did you leave me for Lydia?" he could hear the hurt and emotion in her voice as she spoke.

"I left you for my kids"

"Did you have sex with her?" Why that mattered, she wasn't quite sure, she just wanted to know.

"Yes."

"You broke my heart Ron," her tears overflowed and spilled out onto her cheeks, she wiped them away as quickly as possible.

"I know and I am sorry." He could hear her soft sniffles.

"Why were you so mean to me?" she asked, her eyes still looking straight at the roof of the bathroom.

"I was upset that you moved on, you looked happy with him and I couldn't take it, I admit that it made me feel a little jealous."

"What did you want me to do?"

"I wanted to you to wait for me, as dumb as that sounds, I loved you and I still love you now."

As pretty as she was or as sexy as she was, men still

left her at the drop of a hat.

"I need to be alone."

"Ok," he rapped her on her feet and walked out of the bedroom back to the living room to finish his time with Kareem.

Jessica was tired of men and she was tired of feeling beaten, now her own mother thought she was some cheap trollop, her heart couldn't take anymore, when would she really receive her fairytale ending?

20

Jessica swore off men and over the next two months she focused on Kareem and her work. Kareem was a jubilant nine month old boy, he destroyed everything in her home but the furniture, Jessica had to keep a very close eye on him now that he was able to move around on his own but she loved him dearly, he was everything to her. She was handling being a single mother one day at a time, whenever things got rough and she needed help with him she would either contact Ron or Charmaine. Her relationship with Ron was now strictly platonic. Before, it was only sex to her, nothing more, he wanted to pick up where things left off but she couldn't forget the hell he had put her through.

Before her mother had left, she had apologized for her approach and the harsh words which she said; what her mother said to her really broke her, she wasn't loose by any means, she was a young, single woman free to do whatever she pleased. Anyway, she was no longer sleeping with any of the men she dealt with previously, Timothy eventually got the message and stopped contacting her, she no longer had any uses for him.

The only man she wanted and loved was Trey. She never got over the humiliation she suffered that day at his home when he had rejected her and it sent her heart first back to Ron. Once again another man had broken her heart. Jessica thought long and hard about dating women, how much worse would it be; she'd never been attracted to women, but men weren't working out for her either. Her relationship with Charmaine was still very rocky, they tried to mend fences, but neither wanted to admit that they were wrong. Jessica was sure it was Charmaine that told their mother about her 'choices'. She would tell anyone who would listen that she was grown and what happened in her bedroom was her business. Charmaine would still visit and play with Kareem, however she avoided her sister like the plague.

"My boss is having a dinner party at the Sidonie Restaurant on Friday evening, would you be able to keep Kareem for me?

"Sure"

"I can drop him off when I'm on my way."

"That's fine." That's how their conversations went nowadays, icy and straight to the point, no fluff in between.

Jessica returned to her bedroom, she left Charmaine downstairs with Kareem, she propped up her laptop to eye level and began editing files for work. She didn't want to be in her sister's presence either, when Charmaine was ready to leave she'd yell up the stairs. Jessica could hear Kareem's soft giggles as he played with his aunt, the sound made her smile, the fact that Charmaine was still involved with Kareem, even though they were at odds was satisfying.

Jessica spent the evening of the dinner party looking over her outfit. She chose a beautiful red frilly lace pleated dress that stopped 3 inches above her knees. The sleeves were also designed in the delicate lace which complimented her dark skin perfectly. She decided to pair it with a silver chain and necklace set. She then took a nice shower and nursed Kareem before she applied her makeup.

She sat at her vanity and applied her makeup

meticulously. She was impressed by her talents when she was finished. She turned checking her angles in the mirror before adding moisturizer to her curly hair and stretched it loosely down her shoulders. She slipped into her dress and zipped up the back, that's the one thing she hated about being single, there was no one to zip up her dresses. She hooked her black heels and took one last glance in the mirror with her black clutch dangling at her side. She looked even better than she did before Kareem, all thanks to her exercise sessions and healthy diet. Jessica never stopped working out with her personal trainer, her sessions were held either at her home or at the gym, she often had to push through each grueling session even when she didn't want to, but the benefits she saw were impressive and that motivated her to keep going.

She went into Kareem's room and lifted him gently, trying not to wake him, she held him closely against her chest and scooped up his baby bag and slung it over her shoulder. She cautiously took the stairs and grabbed her car keys from the kitchen counter. Kareem didn't even budge when she strapped him into his seat. She pulled into Charmaine's driveway and honked her horn once and Charmaine soon appeared.

"Damn, he's knocked out."

"Yip. His milk is in the front compartment of his bag."

Charmaine gently took Kareem from his seat, "What time will you be back?"

"Around 10:00 p.m. I guess."

"He can stay over, the boys would love to have him sleep over."

"I'll let you know."

"Cool". Unease surrounded them.

"See you later."

Jessica reversed her car and pulled off, the dinner party was a forty-minute drive. The Restaurant was tucked in the centre of a busy part of town and she had to drive around twice before she found parking just across the street. She exited her car and made her way to the entrance of the restaurant, inside was huge, a portion of it was cordoned off to accommodate the dinner party. A single sign on top of the balcony directed her to the designated area. She greeted her boss and some of her colleagues, they were a few guests she did not know but it wasn't her party so she really didn't care.

She was seated between Syl and Brian and the conversation was some very hot office gossip, Jessica listened intently, offering only the occasional 'hmmm' or 'interesting'.

While she sat listening idly, feigning interest, a waiter approached her with a drink sitting on a tray, he said, "Excuse me miss, your drink is compliments the gentleman at the bar," her eyes followed the direction of his extended finger and to her astonishment, Trey sat at the bar, his hand angled in a salute to her.

"Kindly return it please, I'm a recovering alcoholic." Jessica simply glowered at Trey as the waiter departed. She was not sure if anyone from her office knew she was divorced, but hey, after the information Syl and Brian were throwing her way, they probably already knew, coupled with their exchange just now, she confirmed whatever they were all thinking.

A primal instinct told her to run. She simply wanted to have a little fun tonight not be sequestered in a restaurant across from her ex-husband. Jessica told a quick lie to Syl and Brian that she had to leave urgently, she then found her boss and repeated the same lie before high tailing it out of there and straight to her car.

Before she could physically touch her car, she heard his voice, "Jessica wait," he begged.

He grabbed at her arm, "Don't touch me," as she wrestled away.

He dashed in front of here, his outstretched arms, attempting to slow her down "Just one minute, damn."

She forcefully swatted his hands away from her chest, her stride not breaking for one minute, finally she reached her car and she swung around angrily to face him. "What?" she shouted.

He couldn't find the words to say.

"Ok then, bye." She unlocked her door. Trey ran around to the passenger door and dropped into the passenger seat before she realized and locked her doors.

"How juvenile?" she rolled her eyes aggressively. She could feel her heart racing. From the parking lot, she could see her boss, looking through the big store front window of restaurant directly at her.

"I just want to talk to you," he said, his voice tense.

"You talked to me already, through your divorce papers, remember."

"You have no idea how hard that was for me," he looked at her, his face contorting strangely.

She was sweating. She rolled her windows down, the cool air felt like icicles on her hot skin. "What do you want Trey?" her voice, soft and fragile.

"How is Kareem?

"Don't you dare say his fucking name," she hissed.

An intense standoff ensued.

"I never hated your son Jessica.

"But you hated his mother," she snapped.

"I've never hated you."

"Ok, thanks for that."

"Do you understand the hell you put me through, getting pregnant with your ex's baby, you think it was easy watching his child grow inside of you," his voice went up an octave with every word he spat at her.

Jessica was certain this had to be déjà vu. "Then why are you here, you made your decision and I've left you alone all these months, I understood why you left, I didn't pressure you to stay!" she screamed.

"You won't ever get it, you'll forever be stuck to Ron, he's your son's father!" he shouted.

"I don't have time for this shit," her teeth were clamped so tight, her words were almost indiscernible.

"Have you fucked him since I left?"

"It doesn't matter who I fucked, you left me," she shouted.

"What did you want me to do?" he shouted back.

"This isn't what you want and that's cool, but don't keep shoving the shit in my face every time, I can't take it. Do you want me to my hate my son because of the shit I did, well I can't." Jessica broke down, her eyes burning as the tears rolled down her face, dripping from her chin. "I have apologized over and over and over, Kareem isn't going anywhere and Ron isn't going anywhere, I can't go back in and time and change the past. I accepted your decision long ago, I knew I hurt you, but don't pull me in and then push me away."

"I was hurt too Jess," tears tumbled from his, the pain he felt evident in his voice.

"And you hurt me too." She seriously felt emotionally abused.

102

"I'm sorry Jess, but you needed to get him out of your system for good. I knew you loved him, you wanted to marry him remember, he couldn't have been that bad."

"That was a long time ago. I don't understand you," she eyed him curiously.

"The only way we would have worked out is if you got him out of your system." he wiped his eyes with his fingers.

"So you thought pushing me to him was the right way?" she was flabbergasted.

"I pushed you away so that you would make the decision you needed too, with me gone, you had time to think long and hard about which man you wanted."

"I told you I wanted you." She threw her hands up in the air, she was over it.

"The fact that you went into his house, even after feeling uneasy, that said to me that you kinda sorta wanted ..."

"I didn't want to have sex with him." she stressed.

"All I'm saying is, you didn't have closure with him when he left you and if we were going to work, you needed to see what it was like being with him again, especially with Kareem, you just had a baby for him, that's a bond to him right there."

Jessica dried her face with a tissue from her clutch, "I have to go pick up Kareem." She started her engine.

Trey took the cue and opened the door and stepped out. Jessica pulled off before Trey could close the door, ten minutes into her drive she pulled onto the side of the highway as disgusting cries rumbled from her very soul. She fought for control of her emotions, but she was too weak to stop herself from crying. After thirty minutes, she had calmed down enough to get back on the road to Charmaine's.

21

Jessica made it to Charmaine's driveway, she parked and turned off her engine, she rested her head on her steering wheel, her fingers gripping and wringing around her the cool leather.

The sudden raps on her window, almost gave her a heart attack.

"Why are you back so early?" Charmaine stood watching her sister, Jessica's eyes were red and teary. In seconds, she sat in the passenger's seat.

"What's wrong?" she pulled the hair from her sister's face and tucked it behind her ear. "Jessica, what's wrong?"

"Nothing Char,"

"Whatever it is, you are going to be fine."

Silent tears streamed down her face again.

"Listen, I'll keep Kareem tonight and bring him

back tomorrow."

Jessica agreed, she was not equipped to deal with Kareem right then.

Even though they were at odds, Charmaine was still sympathetic to her sister, she could see that she was going through something. Jessica reversed and headed home, normally she would have spilled her guts to Charmaine, but everyone was judging her character every time she breathed. She kicked off her shoes at the door and went to the kitchen counter, she took five shots of Hennessey to numb her pain, the strong Cognac was so fiery that she wiggled her toes as it went down, she then went into the living room and dropped onto the couch.

She placed the Hennessey bottle on the coffee table, she took one giant swig and laid back on the couch. Jessica was asleep by 10:00 p.m., she woke at 2:00 a.m. and used the bathroom in the powder room and staggered back to the couch and slept until 9:00 a.m.

Her loud noise rattled her brain and one eyed slowly opened. She sprang upright when the thumping sound echoed through her brain again. Jessica opened her eyes, trying to determine where the noise was coming from, her head was pounding terribly as she lifted herself off the couch.

The loud banging on her front door thundered

through her head, she rubbed her eyes and squinted against the sunlight streaming through the windows.

"Alright, I'm coming." she used the walls as a brace as she rocked towards the door.

Jessica didn't even look through the peephole, she just unlocked the door.

Whoever it was walked in behind her.

"Are you drunk?" Trey asked surprised.

"Oh my gosh, dude, leave me alone," she babbled.

Trey took up the almost empty bottle of Hennessy and shook the remaining contents. He went into the kitchen and mixed some weird brew for her to drink.

"Drink this, it'll make you feel better."

"You want to kill me now."

"I don't want to kill you, it'll make you feel better, where's Kareem?" he asked concerned.

"Oh, you care now." She slurred.

"Where the fuck is Kareem?"

"Charmaine's, duhhh."

Jessica was still in her dress from the night before, and she was falling asleep again.

"Jess," he shouted.

"Not so damn loud." she covered her ears with the couch pillow.

"Drink it," he said even louder.

She turned and snatched the cup from his hand, and swallowed the nasty concoction and nestled back into the couch.

While she slept, her cell kept ringing, he found it in her clutch. He answered on the second ring.

"Hey Charmaine, it's me Trey."

"Trey! What are you doing at Jessica's?" He could hear the confusion in her voice. Trey told Charmaine of the conversation between him and Jessica and of the fact that she was drunk and asleep. Charmaine opted to keep Kareem until later in the evening.

Trey stayed with Jessica, while she slept, he palmed her cell around in his hand. He opened her messages, the very first message was to Ron, he opened it, he read the first few words; she was telling him about Kareem, he pushed the cell back into her clutch and sat on the floor next to her.

Jessica stirred around 4:00 p.m. Trey was still on the floor next to the couch.

"Why are you still here? I don't need a babysitter." Damn, she sounded like an old ass man. In her bedroom, she stripped and hit the shower. She lathered and soaped her body as she enjoyed the hot water, she was feeling much better than she did before Trey came bumming down her door. His shitty ass brew did work. She toweled off and dressed and then headed to the kitchen, she was starving, while she cooked, she snacked on grapes and sliced watermelon.

"Charmaine is going to bring Kareem over later, I

told her you were unavailable to speak."

"Ok."

"I didn't mean to offend you last night," he started.

"Can I have some breakfast first?" She muttered numerous expletives under her breath which he still heard.

"It's practically time for dinner," he said sarcastically. She looked at him and rolled her eyes.

"You are here for a reason, I take it?" she was all business.

"I was checking up on you."

"It must be my lucky dayyy," she said dryly.

She took small spoonfuls of her delicious looking chicken stir fry and sat in front of the tv to eat, she switched it on and got comfortable, Trey came and sat next to her, at any other time it would have been pure bliss to have him around, now, he was an awful nuisance she wanted to get rid of.

"You don't have to be a...." he stopped mid-sentence, he was trying to make amends and she was being a spoiled brat.

"A what?..." she wrung her neck from side to side in aggravation. She knew this negro was not about to call her no bitch, she knew that for a fact. She refocused her attention to the television as a breaking news report flashed across the scene.

A snazzily dressed female reporter appeared on

screen, excitedly spilling the details of a salacious story..."the well renowned DNA testing facility is being investigated for several complaints from its wide client base for unscrupulous practices and inappropriate handling of DNA samples..."Jessica could not believe the story, this is where she had her DNA test done, she tried controlling her trembling body and she could feel Trey's eyes boring holes into her, the reporter continued..."The local authorities have halted any and all DNA testing and the facility has been closed temporarily while investigations continue..." What the fuck!

Jessica avoided Trey's stares "What's wrong with you?" he asked.

She crashed her plate on the coffee table, she frantically started searching the couch for her cell, "Move Trey, I need my cell?"

"Got damn Jessica, it's in your bag over there."

Jessica tossed everything from her clutch, she snatched her cell up and ran up the stairs to her bathroom, she slammed the bathroom door shut and sat on the floor, her fingers were shaking and she could hardly punch in her Attorneys number, it took her three tries before she saw the call going through.

"I just saw the news report." Sara answered.

"What does this mean?" she asked, terrified to hear the answer.

"Jessica, I'm sorry, you need to have Trey and Ron retested, just to be sure."

"No. I can't do that again." she cried.

"Jessica, you need to be sure, there's a chance Ron might not be Kareem's father. There is another testing facility, but it's overseas and the results will take a few weeks to come back."

"I don't have the strength to...to start from scratch again."

"Please, think this over, do it for Kareem, he should know who his father is."

"I'll call you next week."

Wait, did Ron really use the same company. She scrambled from the floor and into her closet, she had stuffed the DNA test Ron handed to Trey in a box in her closet. She grabbed the box and threw out the contents on her bed, she ripped through old letters from school and work and other miscellaneous nonsense. She found the bloody sheet of paper stamped with Trey's fingerprints, it was the same company she had used. "Fuck, fuck, fuck." she screamed.

Trey could hear Jessica cursing from the living room, he ran up the stairs and into her bedroom, she was sitting on the bed, lotus style and tons of papers on her thighs, he hurriedly walked over to her shouting "Are you going crazy?"

Jessica was staring into space. Trey snatched the sheet of paper from her hand.

"What the hell is wrong with you?" he asked as he read the contents. It was the DNA test results Ron had slapped on the kitchen island.

"Jessica what the hell is going on?"

"Nothing." He read the paper again.

Then why the hell are you acting cra...," it took him two seconds before he realized why Jessica was acting manic, "Ooh fuck."

22

Jessica wanted Trey out of her sight, his pacing back and forth was driving her up the wall.

"Stop fucking pacing up and down, I need to think."

"What are we going to do?" he asked frowning.

"We?" she shot him a death stare. "Go home Trey," she barked.

Jessica stepped off the bed, the papers on her knees, sailing down to the floor, she took her car key from the kitchen and walked outside. Trey was hot on her heels. She started her engine and pulled away from her curb, she was headed to her spot by the beach. When she had parked and lowered her windows, she noticed Trey sitting in the seat next to her.

113

She sucked air into her lungs, when she saw Trey "What are you doing here?"

"You're really scaring me. Jess, Kareem could be mine," he said softly.

"Trey, I can't handle your sorrows along with mine," she said gloomily.

"We need a new DNA test."

"I know," she smiled. She was insanely tired of crying so she smiled.

"Man, do you know what that would mean for us?" he exclaimed.

"It wouldn't mean anything," her eyes fixed on his, "you've never forgiven me for sleeping with Ron, whether Kareem is yours or not, you checked out."

"I'd be willing to try."

"Oh for fucks sake, get out." She seethed.

She wished he would go away.

"Jessica," he began.

She didn't want to hear anything he had to say, "It took me a long while to be ok with being divorced and a single mother." Her gaze returned to the view of the beach.

"I never stopped loving you."

"Mmmm."

He cupped her chin in his hand, turning her to face him.

"I meant what I said, I never stopped loving you, I

did what I thought was best."

She tugged her chin away. "I did love you too but I'm tired of begging you to love me, I acknowledged my mistake with Ron, but I won't spend the rest of my life paying for it. I love my son no matter who his father is.

Her cell rang, "Hello," it was Charmaine, she was headed over to Jessica's with Kareem.

"I'll be home shortly." She switched on her engine, closed her windows and turned on the air condition and backed out of the parking space. Charmaine sat outside in her car waiting for Jessica when she pulled up at the curb. She took her key from the ignition and locked her doors while Trey walked over to Charmaine's car. She had a bouncing Kareem in her arms. Jessica ran up to Kareem and smothered him with kisses, he held on to her face trying to nibble her nose, he was happy to see his mother too.

"Thank you for keeping him overnight," Jessica said, unease washing over her.

"He's my nephew, I'd do anything for him," she said as she ran her hand over his curly hair.

"Can we talk?"

"Sure."

They all bundled into the living room, Jessica sat and bounced Kareem on her knees to his delight. Charmaine and Trey sat on the bigger couch together,

Kareem soon started fussing and stretching, trying to get on the floor, something had caught his attention.

"Let's go on the patio," Jessica said to Charmaine.

"I can hold him until you guys are finished talking," Trey piped up.

Jessica paused, not sure what to do, she handed a wiggling Kareem to Trey. When Kareem noticed the exchange to Trey, he simply stared into his face and his awkward hand movement smacked Trey right in mouth.

"Good boy." Jessica cheered to which Charmaine smacked her hard on her arm.

"Don't tell him that!" she said irritated.

"Sorry." Jessica was not close to sorry, but she said it for Charmaine's benefit. Charmaine closed the patio door before sitting opposite Jessica on the patio bench, they both were looking straight ahead at the evening traffic milling by.

"I want to apologize for the way I acted the last time we talked."

"You were right, I was judging you and I'm sorry."

"Your opinion of me really matters and I hated to know that I disappointed you. At that time, I was reeling over Trey's rejection, I was divorced and a single mother, it was soo much that I was maybe trying to find love wherever I found it."

"I know that but when you began to run that mouth,

girllll I couldn't take that shit, your mouth can be lethal." Charmaine chuckled. "I have a pretty good idea what it's like to find love under another man, it's no picnic when you come down off of that high."

Jessica sighed.

"Why is Trey here?" Charmaine whispered to Jessica.

"Girl my life is a shit storm; a comedy show, it's like I can't catch a break.

Jessica gave Charmaine a quick rundown on the shenanigans of her life, she first started with her and Trey's exchange from last night and ended with the DNA facility malpractice debacle. Jessica did not tell Charmaine that she had used the same company to conduct her own personal test done. She was taking that one to her grave.

"So you came home and got wasted."

"Correct, I couldn't deal with him or that. I didn't want to feel anything, numb from head to toe."

"Damn, you were going through it."

"Sara thinks I should get them both retested."

"And?"

"And I don't want to go through that again, there's too much emotion involved, the stress of not knowing and then the men involved."

"Just do it and get it over with."

"I'm scared."

117

"You need to let them both know and make your stance on the outcome clear."

"I just want to move on, it feels like I'm constantly on a rollercoaster ride between two men.

Kareem started banging on the door and he staggered outside when Charmaine opened the door. When he lost his balance and dropped straight onto his butt, he crawled over to his mother and stretched his arms out. Jessica lifted him up and he immediately tried getting into her shirt. Jessica slipped her top and bra down so that he could nurse before she remembered she was drunk as hell moments ago. She asked Trey to collect his expressed milk from the refridgerator, he returned and stood by the patio door watching Kareem drink from his bottle, Kareem was enthralled with the stranger at the door, he stopped feeding and sat up in his mother's lap, he fussed at Trey and then laid back and continued drinking his milk.

"What was that about Trey?" Charmaine laughed.

"I have no idea," he smiled.

Charmaine soon returned home, leaving Trey and Jessica alone. Not long after feeding Kareem he went down for his nap. Jessica burped him over her shoulder and then took him to his cradle, he was going to be asleep for a long while. She returned and sat on the couch and Trey joined her, sitting very close to her.

"He's a wonderful boy."

"Thanks."

"I really hope he's mine," he looked away before she could see the tears in his eyes.

Jessica scooped all of her hair into a top knot bun, "What if he's not," she said, then we are back at square one and I'm left to pick up the pieces."

"I won't leave this time."

"Hmmm, now where have I heard that before," she scoffed, "Don't worry, I'm not holding your feet to the fire."

He didn't like that comment, "I think I should go."

"Ever since," she muttered beneath her breath.

"Walk me out."

Jessica stood and opened the door, she stepped back giving him enough space to pass by. Trey walked directly into her personal space and began kissing her, it was so sudden that her lips automatically responded, her hand dropped from the door knob and cradled his face. He lifted her up, pressing her into the wall, she wrapped her legs around his waist as his agile fingers groped her breasts through her shirt, a quick flash of the divorce papers flying at his head pierced through her brain and she broke away from him, pushing him off, "I can't do this," she breathed, he dropped her legs and they stood face to face, breathing hard, he slowly backed away, his erection evident, by the huge bulge in

119

his pants, which she noticed and looked in the other direction.

"Keep me posted on the DNA test."

"Great."

Jessica trudged back to the couch. Her decision was final, she was indeed going to become a lesbian, men were too complicated. She took out her laptop and researched recognized DNA testing facilities. She spent over an hour online searching and reading as much information as she could. She dreaded speaking to Ron about retesting him, but she needed to get the process going, it was only 8:00 p.m., hopefully he was still awake, she punched in Ron's number and waited for him to answer.

"Hey, uhhh can you come over tonight?"

"Is something wrong with Kareem?"

"No, Kareem is fine, but we need to talk, it would be better in person"

"Ok, I'll be there soon."

Ron arrived forty minutes later, he was almost running to her door.

"What's so urgent that we need to talk tonight?"

She patted the seat next to her on the couch and he sat glaring at her, waiting anxiously for her to continue. Jessica pulled up an online article about the DNA testing centre now under investigation.

"Once you read this you will understand." She

observed the lines and drawn features on Ron's face as he read the article.

"Is this legit?"

"Yes, I saw it on the news."

"Damn."

"I need to have you retested."

"Shit."

"I would like to set it up as soon as possible."

"This is beyond ridiculous.

I'm going to ask Sara to arrange to have it done privately, that way we can all arrange an appropriate date and time to give our samples.

"Fine. How do you feel about it?"

"I'm scared." She said.

He rubbed her shoulders. "We'll get through this."

"Can I see him before I go?"

"Sure." They walked up to Kareem's room, silently, each in their own worlds.

Ron stroked his legs with his finger, Kareem stretched and kicked slightly. She noticed the tears rolling from his eyes. He bent and kissed Kareem and turned to her, wiping his face with his shirt.

"Thanks Jess," he said and headed down the stairs and out to his car. Jessica was mentally and emotionally shattered.

She went downstairs and checked that Ron had locked her door. She flipped her lights off and returned to her bedroom. She switched the tv on and tried to focus on something other than the trouble brewing all around her.

23

J essica held a wiggling Kareem snuggly on her lap, Trey and Ron sat on opposite ends of the room, waiting for the medical professional to swab them for the DNA tests. They each were interviewed individually and their personal information collected and inserted into a database. Ron went first, then Trey, then Jessica and their individual swabs were placed in a clear bag and sealed.

The paternity results were to be sent to Sara, Jessica's Attorney at which time they would all meet at her office for the results to be read. Directly after the samples were taken neither Ron nor Trey knew where Jessica disappeared to, she was already pulling out of the carpark of the facility and on her way home. She placed Kareem on the floor and stopped to take off her shoes, Kareem, at ten months old, was far advanced compared to other babies his age. He followed Jessica to the kitchen where she washed her hands while he held onto her leg to pull himself up to a standing position, he wobbled his way around her legs to pull open one of the cabinet drawers and when his mother said "No baby," he released the knob and moved to a new drawer, Jessica swiped him from the floor and took him to her bedroom, where she changed into comfy shorts and tube top.

As soon as Kareem saw her breasts, he started to fuss so she scooped him into her arms and fed him, she wanted to wean Kareem from nursing, his two bottom teeth made it painful for her to feed, he gnawed her nipple most times he fed, once Kareem was full he wiggled from her hands and crawled to each bedside table and pushed everything on the table to the floor, just as he pulled the lamp, she stopped him and sat him between her legs and tossed a couple toys around him to keep him occupied. Jessica switched the tv on and at the sound coming from the big black box hung from the wall, his attention switched from his toys to the pretty colors on the tv.

She took her cell and began scrolling through her favorite gossip sites, there was nothing of interest happening so she decided to watch a few YouTube videos. Within twenty minutes, Kareem was asleep, as she stroked his legs it became apparent to her that Kareem's life could possibly be changing once more, did she want it to change? No not really, Ron was really a good dad, he and Kareem had bonded as father and son, she had to give thanks that the story of the DNA facility came out when it did, even though it complicated everything, at least it happened while he was still a baby and not as a teen or adult, she wouldn't know what to do if she found out her father was not her father, she wondered if Kareem would think she was a whore if he ever found out the circumstances surrounding the whole DNA fiasco.

Hopefully, he would never hear of the confusion surrounding his conception. She needed to make a decision on what she would need to do if Trey was found to Kareem's biological father. Damn, she felt like she was on Maury. As much as she wanted Trey before, it simply wasn't the same, sure, she loved him but was she *in* love with him, they had been through so much, he probably wouldn't even trust her to walk a straight line down the street, not that it mattered, but she was sick of men and sick of the shit they brought her way.

The two weeks it took for the results to return were the most nerve-wracking weeks she had ever experienced, her life had literally stopped, she took a few days off and opted to work from home, she honestly wanted to hide under a rock until she knew who was Kareem's father, she was functioning at fifty percent and she really didn't care. Ron seldom visited Kareem, he was afraid of the outcome and the emotional torture it would cause him if he was not his father, he would however, video call Jessica and baby babble with Kareem occasionally, he thought it best to wait and pray that nothing would have to change.

Trey, like Jessica, was unable to function, he again hunkered down in his home, waiting and praying, he wasn't sure what he was praying for. His biggest regret would be divorcing Jessica, at that time, he was fueled by his pain and anger towards her, he wasn't sure if she was intimate with Ron but he suspected she had, especially after he humiliated her when she initiated sex with him, it was only human nature. While he was stewing in his thoughts, he saw Cameron pull into his driveway, from through his open windows.

He got up and opened the door; he left it wide open for his buddy to come through. Cameron brought two six packs of beer and sat them on the coffee table.

"You look like shit bro." They smacked hands together and Cameron sat in the chair opposite Trey, "No offense."

"None taken." Trey replied unbothered.

"Man I listened to your voice note twice while coming over here and that shit is wild."

Trey took a beer from the pack and popped the cap. "I can't even think properly."

"What are you going to do if he's yours?"

"What do you think I'm going to do?" he said tightlipped.

"I told you not to divorce her man!" he said pointing a finger at Trey.

"What was I supposed to do?" he gulped a mouthful of beer.

"You stick by your got damn wife, you make it work, make rules and arrange how Ron's visits happen, you respectfully ask your wife to set guidelines where he can't go all over your house; he can't come in the house or if he comes in the house, yuh know, he has a set area to play with Kareem and then when he gets older Kareem can go over to his house that way Ron doesn't have to come into your house anymore."

"Easier said than done," Trey mocked.

"There were ways man, you just didn't wanna fucking listen and now she doesn't want your ass cause you pushed her away."

"You are always on her side."

"Now that's fucked up, I give unbiased ass opinions nigga, now you have to start from scratch."

"Nigga fuck you."

"You sent her packing when she came looking for some 'buddy', if I was her I'd pay your ass dust too." Cameron held his stomach as he doubled over laughing.

Trey was glaring at Cameron, "I didn't invite you over to ridicule me man"

"True dat," Cameron took a beer from the pack, "What games are on?"

"I haven't been watching anything." He tossed the remote to Cameron and popped another beer.

Trey's mind was swirling as he watched Cameron animatedly react to the plays on his giant 50 inch tv screen. He wanted to be a father, he was optimistic about the outcome of the DNA results, but he was well aware that Ron was proven to be Kareem's father once, it could happen again. He was willing to do anything in his power to win his wife back, well, if she would have him.

Jessica got the call everyone was waiting for. She had arranged with Sara to meet at her office at 1:00 p.m. that Thursday. Her, Trey and Ron all sat in front of Sara's desk staring at the brown envelopes in front of them, it was like looking at bombs about to explode and there was no place to duck for cover. She zoned out as Sara demonstrated to each person sitting before her that the two envelopes were all sealed and were in no way tampered with. Sara opened the tab of the first envelope and delicately pulled the papers from the envelope and she then opened the tab of the second envelope. The bile from Jessica's guts bubbled up in her throat, she knew the two men beside her had to be shitting bricks. Trey stealthily held her hand as the results were read, suddenly he dropped her hand, and as she looked at him quizzically, she saw his tear filled eyes looking back at her.

Jessica heard Sara say "Do each of you understand the documents as I have read them to you?"

No one answered.

"Any questions?" she asked again.

"No. Thank you," Ron said, he lowered his face in his hands, fear racing through his veins.

"Jessica?" Sara called.

"Uhnmm no, thank you." Jessica handed Sara a cheque in exchange for the envelopes.

"You are most welcome and thank you also."

They all filed out of Sara's office. Jessica adjusted Kareem on her shoulder as she headed to the carpark. After she had secured Kareem, she pulled the envelopes from her purse and read the information again and again until it sunk in. The words 'probability of paternity' flashed like an 'open' sign in her mind constantly, she couldn't shake the image regardless of what she occupied her mind with, she started her engine and checked her surroundings before pulling out of the space, she didn't see Ron nor Trey, she didn't want to see them either.

At home, Jessica stared at a sleeping Kareem, searching his face for traces of his father, she found nothing. He was her twin, from his curly black hair to the color of his dark skin. She kissed his forehead and returned to her bedroom. Jessica turned her cell off and laid back in her bed, she didn't want to speak to anyone or see anyone. She needed a moment before she had to face reality.

She fluffed her pillows and laid back, how were two DNA tests wrong, she thought, it boggled her mind. Obviously, no one knew of the test she had done, it didn't make sense to her. She changed positions to rest her cheek on her hands. She soon fell into a fitful sleep, tossing and turning, her body unable to relax. After ten minutes of restless sleep, she was out of bed, she had to do something. She flopped into bed as a simple thought came to mind.

Jessica laid in the center of the bed and spread her legs, she slid her hands into her shorts and between her legs, she began to caress the soft supple flesh of her womanhood, the more she worked her fingers, the wetter she became, she slipped her fingers deep inside of her and briskly massaged her walls, she withdrew her moist fingers and rubbed her clit until she felt the tickle of her climax peak, she moaned deed within her throat as she came, her walls gripping at nothing but air.

"Jessica, what the hell are you doing?" Charmaine shouted, stunned.

"Go away Charmaine." Jessica sighed as her legs trembled slightly, she didn't even acknowledge her sister.

"Oh my gosh," she covered her eyes with her hand, "bitch hurry up and come down stairs." She was utterly disgusted.

Jessica pulled out her fingers from her slit and chuckled, this was not the first time Charmaine had walked in on her pleasing herself, many moons ago, when they lived at home with their parents, she had walked into Jessica's room without knocking, for a while after that she learned to knock.

Jessica cleaned herself up and washed her hands before meeting her sister downstairs, she pretended to pick up a pillow from the couch and glided her fingers across Charmaine's face as she walked by. A swift kick to the back of her leg brought her down.

"Ouch," she said laughing, "You could have broken my leg," she said between fits of laughter.

"Don't ever do that again!" Charmaine felt repulsed

and stood to kick her again.

"Ok! ok!, I washed my hands," she sniffed her fingers, 'clean', she said.

Charmaine sucked her teeth.

"How'd you get in here anyway?"

"I used the spare key." After they had made up, Jessica returned the spare key to her home to Charmaine.

"Why didn't you just knock?"

"I did bitch and you didn't answer?"

"I didn't hear you."

"Obviously. So what happened today?" she asked gleefully.

Jessica ran to her purse and snatched up the envelopes and tossed them to Charmaine. She read both papers before replacing them in their respective envelopes.

"This reminds me of how humans will chop down a tree and then write, 'save the trees' on the same got damn paper." They looked at each other before ferocious laughter consumed them.

24

Jessica worked from home three weeks after she received the results. There was no way she could possibly focus on work when her life was turned upside down. Trey came over every evening and visited with Kareem from the moment he was declared his father. Kareem was a tad hesitant at first, he screamed the house down whenever Trey picked him up so she had to be present whenever they interacted, if she ever left the room, he'd crawl or stagger behind her but day by day he became a little more comfortable with Trey.

He'd calmly sit and play with Trey until he got hungry or tired. Trey showered him with toys, food, clothes, anything he could think of, he brought over.

Her office was once again stuffed with baby items.

"Trey, some of these things he can't use until he's at least two years old."

"That's fine, I can store them at my house until then."

"That's fine with me."

"He has a ton of energy, wow."

"I feel for the nannies at the nursery." Jessica stretched out on the floor with Kareem in the middle of her and Trey, "When he gets home, he roams until he's ready to sleep or feed."

"You guys could move in with me." He knew it was too soon, but he didn't really care, they were apart too long.

"You guys could move...." Kareem took his toy ball from the floor and dropped it in Trey's lap and Trey took him in his arms and kissed his cheek.

She stopped him, "I heard what you said."

"It'd make it easier on you, since I can easily pick him up."

"I pick him up just fine thank you."

"I wanna spend more time with him."

"What do you call this?" she asked rudely.

"You know what I mean, I want him in the same home as me."

"I'm not ready for that."

"How do you feel about the results?"

"I need like a good year of overwhelming happiness. I feel like I've been through hell this last year and I want him to be happy."

"And Ron?" he asked very interested in her answer.

"And Ron, what?" she wasn't following him.

"Where do you stand with him?" He was playing with Kareem's hair while looking directly at her.

"Ask me what you really want to ask me?" she looked over at him.

"Were you having sex with him?"

"No, I wasn't." Damn! Another secret she was taking to her grave.

"Is that the truth?"

"If I'm lying I'm flying."

"Hmmm."

"Does it really matter? We weren't together at the time."

"Fair enough."

"Can I stay over and spend more time with him?" he flashed a big smile.

"You can stay a little longer but you can't sleep over." She was having mixed emotions. She was almost positive she was no longer in love with Trey, now, being so close to him, she was unsure, she didn't want him to stay over because she knew what would happen if he did and at that moment she didn't have the strength to stop him.

Kareem stumbled over to his mother, his little hands tugging at her bra, she sat up and freed her breast to feed him and as usual he palmed her free breast with his hand.

"Why does he do that?" Trey chuckled.

"Beats me, he only does it when he's nursing"

"Hmm," Trey scooted down onto the floor next to Jessica, he held Kareem's little finger, Kareem stopped and looked at Trey before returning to his mother's breast.

"Do you still leak milk when you cum?"

Jessica looked at Trey dubiously, ignoring the slight quiver between her legs at the thought of him licking the milk from her breasts.

"Were you sleeping with anyone while you were single?" He asked her so, fair is fair.

"Do you really want to know?"

"I asked didn't I?"

"Yes."

"Who?"

"It doesn't matter."

"Hmmm, are you still having sex with this person?"

"No, it was a casual fling."

"Great," she flashed him an awkward smile.

He rubbed her arms lightly, his fingers tracing a single line up and down, "I'm really serious about you guys moving in with me."

"I love my own house."

"At least think about it."

Oh my gosh, the more she looked into his eyes, the more her strength waned.

Trey helped Jessica from the floor, Kareem had fallen asleep and she couldn't get off the floor.

"Let me take him up," he offered.

"Ok." She sat on the couch and switched the tv from the game he was watching, she soon found an interesting fight live on some reality tv. Trey returned fifteen minutes later.

"He looks soo peaceful when he's asleep."

"That's until he wakes up screaming the whole house down," she laughed.

"I've got an early start tomorrow so I'm gonna head out."

"See you tomorrow."

"Remember to call his nursery and let them know, that uhh Ron won't be picking him anymore," his demeanor very candid.

"Yea, I haven't forgotten."

When she was finally alone, she contacted Ron, she knew he was feeling like shit and she felt awful.

"Hey, how are you?"

"I'm cool, considering, how is Kareem?"

"He's great, thanks,"

"I miss him Jess, it's hard," the pain in his voice

evident.

"I'm so sorry Ron," she sniffled, wiping her eyes with her top.

Jessica heard the mournful cry released from his soul, "I loved him so much."

"I know you loved him and he loved you," she said sadly, "I'm sorry Ron."

"I am too. I felt so lucky to have a second chance," she heard him blowing his nose.

"I know."

"Do you think Trey would let me see him some times."

"No fucking way," she blurted out.

Ron chuckled. "I wouldn't blame him."

"I can send you photos of him so you can see how amazing he's growing."

"Thank you."

"Jess before you go, I have to ask...maybe I shouldn't, if you don't want to answer I will understand..."

"I honestly don't know. I can say that you were an awesome father to Kareem and I appreciate the way you stepped up to help take care of him."

"Thank you."

"You come by tomorrow after work, say goodbye to him."

"What about Trey?"

"I'll handle him."

"Thank you. I will be there around 5:00 p.m."

25

Before she lost her nerve, she called Trey to give him a heads up about Ron coming over.

"Hi Jess."

"Listen," she breathed before continuing, "I invited Ron to see Kareem later, for him to sort of say goodbye."

"Why?"

"Because, he spent the last ten months being his dad, I think he needs closure."

"Is that so? He paused...Fine, what time is he coming?"

"5:00 p.m."

"Cool, I'll be there."

"Trey..." He disconnected the call.

Trey was not about to let Ron visit with his son unsupervised, call him paranoid, but he did not trust Ron at all and Jessica was not going to make that decision for him.

Jessica was annoyed that he hung up on her, she didn't need Trey to oversee Ron's visit, she could handle Ron alone. He wasn't bothered about Ron when he had divorced her. She pushed them both from her mind and refocused on her work. Her itinerary was full and by the end of the day, she was extremely tired. She collected Kareem and adjusted her rearview mirror so that she could see him while he watched a cartoon from the tv monitor she had mounted on the back of the passenger seat.

When she pulled up to her curb, Trey was already there. He got out of his car and removed Kareem from his seat. He kissed and hugged him while Jessica grabbed the bags from the trunk.

"You don't have to be here," she said walking past him.

"I don't have to but I want too."

Jessica unlocked the front door and kicked her shoes off, Trey took Kareem into the living room and started playing with him. Kareem was at the stage that the world was his oyster and he tasted everything with his mouth and his father's face was no exception. She texted Ron quickly alerting Ron that Trey was there also, she really didn't want any issues between the both of them.

Ron arrived a little after 5:00 p.m., he had received Jessica's text so he wasn't surprised to see Trey. He greeted them both and headed to the patio and Jessica held Kareem's hand as he waddled out to Ron. Kareem instantly remembered Ron and staggered over to him, Ron lifted him up and sat him on his knees. He smelled his hair, rubbed his chest and he hugged him gently. He didn't intend to stay long, he just wanted a few minutes with him to say goodbye. After kissing him on his forehead and speaking to him in hushed tones, he passed him back to Jessica and headed for the floor.

Jessica snatched the cheque from her purse and ran after Ron, she caught him outside of his car, "Wait," when she looked at him, there were tears flowing down his face. She handed it to him, "It's the support money you gave me before."

"You don't have to pay this back to me."

"Under the circumstances, it's your money."

"You have two options; you can put it in a bank account for him until he gets older or you can give it to charity.

She stood with her hand still outstretched. "I don't want the money back Jess."

"Ok."

He turned and got into his car and peeled away from the curb. Jessica watched his car disappear in the distance and when she could only see his tail lights, she walked back to her door. Trey stood in the entry way watching her with Kareem cradled against his chest.

She strode inside feeling defeated. She remembered him expressing wanting another chance to raise more children if he was ever given the opportunity and she felt bad for him. She personally couldn't bare further disappointment; so much had happened in her love life that she prayed for no more surprises. Kareem reached out for her when she stepped into the doorway, she propped him on her hip and walked into the living room while stuffing the cheque into the pocket of her shorts.

"I'm gonna go give him a bath."

"What's for dinner?"

"Leftovers."

"I'll whip us up something real quick."

While she undressed him on the bed, Jessica filled the tub with enough water for his bath. She grabbed a towel and placed it under her knees from the hard floor and   tossed in a few toys and sat him in the centre of the tub. With Kareem splashing around his toys in the water, it gave her the opportunity to wash his hair, which he hated, so she had to move fast before he noticed what she was doing. She pulled his towel from the rack and quickly swaddled him without getting her own clothing soaked. He smelt so fresh and clean. She dried him and dressed him in his pajamas and took him back to the living room.

"Dinner will be ready in two minutes."

"What did you cook?"

"I did a kale salad with fried salmon."

Jessica placed Kareem on his mat and stood by the kitchen watching him play with his toys.

"That's it between him and Kareem?"

"Yes." Jessica rolled her eyes, men can be so territorial.

Kareem staggered into the kitchen and pulled Trey's pants, reaching out his little hands for Trey to take him up.

"How do you feel about me being Kareem's dad?"

"I can't change the results of the test, I can only adapt to the situation."

"That's your politically correct answer, now I want the truth."

"That is *the* truth," she sighed.

They sat on the couch eating and passing small bites to Kareem before things got serious.

"I would like to move back in."

"You don't need to move back in to spend time with Kareem. He's old enough to spend the weekends with you."

"I want us to live under the same roof."

"I need you to give me time. I'm not ready for anything more."

"I respect that."

"You what irks me, is that I loved you so much. It ripped my soul to shreds when you left, and you left me alone with a young baby and you didn't look back. The funny thing is, if Ron was his dad, you wouldn't even be here."

He placed Kareem into his swing and turned the mobile on. "Ok, let's get this shit all out once and for all, after this, we are not going back to it ever."

Trey and Jessica went head to head, battling each other furiously, hurt for hurt, pain for pain, when they had spilled everything on their hearts, the room was silent and tense. Jessica understood why he left and why he was hurt. They hurt each other; she felt no ill will towards him and him none for her.

"Anything else you need me to answer."

"No."

"Good," he took her hands in his, "I would love for us to start over."

"I'm so scared of getting hurt again," she said softly.

"I won't ever hurt you again. We deserve a second chance, please don't throw away what we had," he pleaded.

She looked at him squarely in his eyes before

sudden tears tumbled from her eyes, "You hurt me Trey, you abandoned and rejected me."

"I'm sorry, if I knew better I would have done better." She cried on his shoulders for a few minutes and when she was done, her face was red with embarrassment.

"We can do this," he insisted.

26

"Where's Trey?" Charmaine asked.
"Carters."

"How come?"

"That's where he lives Char."

"Thought you said he wanted you to move back in."

"I need some more time." Jessica and Charmaine were at the beach with the kids. Kareem stayed close to his mother, the big vast water scared him and he simply watched as the waves crashed against the shore.

"Are you guys having sex?"

"No," she snapped.

"I'm just asking, jeez."

"I'm not there yet."

"I guess you handle your business yourself," she

said sarcastically.

Jessica twinkled her fingers at her sister and laughed.

Charmaine made a face at Jessica, "You brought it up," Jessica huffed.

"Have you given any thought to moving to Carters?"

"Yea, but I'm not feeling that, I love my home," she said adjusting her sunglasses over her eyes.

"It's not just you anymore Jess."

"I'm aware of that. His mother called me, she said she knew we were meant to be together, people make mistakes, she can't wait to hold her grandson, yadda, yadda, yadda."

"That's nice of her," she paused, "Do you hear from Ron?"

"Nope."

"I know he loved Kareem, it must be hard for him."

"It is. I promised him I'd send him pics of Kareem occasionally," she averted her eyes from her sister's nasty glare.

"Does Trey know?" she shrieked.

"Why would he need to know?"

"I think you need to discuss this with him, it's his son, and he needs to be comfortable with you sending your ex-lover pics of his son."

Jessica cut her eyes at her sister. Charmaine was right and she knew it. She just wasn't ready to have that particular conversation with Trey after they had put all of their issues on the table.

"Maybe, maybe not," she fed Kareem water from his bottle and rested him between her thighs.

Jessica took Kareem for a dip in the water. He gripped her swimsuit top tightly and refused to let the water touch his little feet. Jessica cupped water in her hand and poured it over his knees and that still didn't stop him from clinging to her, she returned to the lounge chairs after too many failed attempts. Kareem slid out of her arms and started playing in the sand. Charmaine passed her a container stacked with a variety of sandwiches and she took two and ate them slowly while feeding Kareem pieces as he played in the sand until it was time to go.

When they got home after their day at the beach, Jessica bathed Kareem and fed some fruit and water and once he went down for his nap, she made herself a cup of tea and caught up on her reality tv, Trey came over just as she was cleaning up the kitchen, in his hands he held three grocery bags full of food and snacks for Kareem.

"Listen, I need to talk to you about something."

He came over and rested the bags on the counter, "What's up?"

She searched the bags and began putting away the items, she hid her face behind the open cabinet door,

"I told Ron that I would send him pics of Kareem every once in a while"

"For what reason?" he asked to the cabinet door.

"Because he had a bond with Kareem and he was his dad for a very long time."

"I don't care what he *was*, he's not getting pics of my son as mementos."

She slammed the cabinet door shut. "It's really not that serious."

"Great, well you can send him pics of you if you want," he snapped.

"Ohh that was low."

"Are you ever going to let him go?"

"What the fuck is that supposed to mean?" she barked.

"No matter how hard we try to get him out of our lives, you want to drag his ass back in."

"That not fair."

"I'm sick and tired of this shit."

"You don't have to stay, the door is right over there," she pointed a finger at the door.

"You *were* fucking him, weren't you? 'Cause what you're saying doesn't make sense."

"If I fucked him or when I fucked him is none of your got damn business," her heart was racing; her peaceful day had now turned to shit.

He scowled at her before heading upstairs into

Kareem's room.

"Fuck!" she felt bad for what she'd said to him, sending the pics to Ron wasn't a way to keep him around, at least not in her opinion.

She grabbed her cell and went out onto the patio. When Charmaine answered she went straight into her rant.

"We got into it again, he thinks I want to send Ron pics of Kareem as a way to keep him close and that's truly not it.

"I can see why he'd think that."

"But, that's not the case."

"Are you sure?"

"Yes," she shouted.

"Look, if he doesn't want Ron to have his son's pics, give him that respect and don't do it.

She sighed loudly, "I guess you're right."

"Gotta go sissy, thanks," Jessica slipped her cell into her pocket and stood at the bottom of the stairs, she didn't know what she was going to say to Trey but she had to start somewhere.

Trey was resting on the bed in Kareem's room, his eyes were open, staring at the ceiling. He looked at her when she pushed the door open but said nothing. She peeked at Kareem and sat on the edge of the bed, "I'm sorry, I won't send any pics of Kareem to Ron and I swear I'm not trying to keep him close or have a way to contact him."

Trey didn't budge or respond, she stared at him long and hard before she left the room "Do you want him or me?" she heard him ask.

"To be honest, I don't want neither him *nor* you."

27

Of course she didn't mean it, she wanted to hurt him for hurting her feelings, she was trying and she didn't appreciate his snide remarks. Jessica's heart skipped a beat when he burst through her bedroom. She sat up as he stalked over to her, glaring at her from the side of the bed. He snapped his belt off and shoved his boxers and jeans to his feet and kicked them off and flung his shirt over his head, he stood at her feet naked and hard and she caught herself ogling his engorged erection.

Suddenly, he grabbed both of her legs and dragged her to the edge of the bed, even though this wasn't their first time having sex; she felt like a virgin, afraid yet excited to be ravished by her lover. The look in his eyes made her slit cream as she relished in the thought of him ravishing her. He stripped her out of her clothing and climbed over her and spread her legs open. A low shaky moan escaped her lips when the tip of his shaft pressed against her moist slit. For fourteen minutes, she thought Trey was going to kill her, his hammering of her slit was ferocious and ravenous, her body convulsed against the sweet pounding rhythm between her legs, she screamed "wait, shitttt" just as he rested on his arms, giving himself better leverage to drive his swollen shaft deeper inside of her "No," he said, his breath caught in his throat and she hugged his waist tightly with her thighs, trying to control the depth of his strokes.

Jessica knew he was punishing her for her slick ass mouth and before she knew it, she was face down on the bed using the pillows to muffle her passionate cries, she was aware that Kareem was asleep in the next room and did not want to wake him. The slapping sounds of his body against her soft flesh titillated her even more.

"Got damn, you are so fucking wet," he growled, the rich smell of their sex wetting his appetite for more, Jessica was not normally turned on by 'dirty talk' but his words, coupled with the exquisite beating of her walls, sent her body into a frenzy and her juices slowly seeped out of her in tiny squirts.

She gasped loudly as he gripped her waist tighter,

driving his hard length to the hilt, she inhaled sharply as rockets exploded behind her eyes and flutters of electricity pulsated from her slit to every nerve ending of her body, just then, he swiftly held her hands behind her back with one hand and spread her legs wider with the other, her head flew back as his rapid fire thrusts buckled her legs and her body bucked and jerked against him; forget not waking Kareem, the immoral moans she yelped could wake the dead, a prickly heat shot through her clit and she tried closing her legs but he wouldn't let her, he increased his rhythm and fucked the shit out of her from behind, her grunting and groaning became animalistic and the sweet throbbing between her legs forced her walls to contract intensely and streaks of her juices slinked down her thighs, "Oh yessss, baby," she heard him say.

The product from her sweaty hair was burning her eyes and her body was about to go limp, her legs shaked uncontrollably and she could feel his sweat dripping onto her back. Trey held her against him and she couldn't move, the harder he thrust into her, the more she inched away. Moments later she found herself hanging off of the bed, her arms the only things keeping her from falling. "Baby don't' move," her breathing was choppy and short, Trey fucked her in that position until he came, an airy wheeze belted out of him as he emptied all of his anger, hurt and frustration inside of her, his expanding shaft spurting and jerking his cum from his trembling body, he released her and she fell right off the bed. Trey couldn't even help her, he collapsed on the bed after her spent.

Neither person could move. Jessica's body felt hot as wave after wave of pre climax pleasure travelled through her centre which was numb and swollen. After a few short minutes, her spasms had abated, but she still couldn't move.

"Baby did you drop off the bed?"

"Yes," she laughed, "And now I can't move." Trey staggered off the bed and lay next to her on the floor.

"Are you hurt?" Jessica couldn't believe he'd ask her that after nearly destroying her womanhood.

"You really gonna ask me that after just now?" Jessica's face was hidden by her wild mane, "Try another question."

He moved her hair back, "I don't have another one," he groped her butt before planting a kiss just at the curve of her hips.

She turned on her side and looked at him. "I really can't move Trey."

He rubbed her thighs and smiled. "Ok, I'll go check on Kareem."

"There's a camera right there," she pointed to the monitor on her bedside table. He peeped over the bed and saw that Kareem was still asleep. Jessica stayed on the floor for another fifteen minutes before she grabbed a hold of the bed covers and pulled herself up while Trey went to shower.

She walked into the bathroom and opened the cabinet door looking for antiseptic for her scraped knee. Trey stepped out of the stall and embraced her warmly when something caught his eye. He pulled a circular container from one of the shelves and held it to her face.

"Birth Control?"

She snatched it from his hands and tossed it back into the cabinet and closed the door and then stepped into the shower.

When she returned to the bedroom, Trey sat on the bad, silent.

"I was on birth control but I stopped taking it months ago," she said, "Besides I was a single woman."

"I understand," he pecked her on her cheek, "Meet me downstairs."

Jessica caught a glimpse of movement from the camera on her table, Kareem was up. She dried herself quickly and went into his room, when he saw her, he stretched out his hands for her to pick him up and once he was in her arms, he instantly tried nursing through her top.

"Ok, ok," she chuckled.

She held him in one hand and took him into the living room with her, she sat on the couch and pulled her top down so he could feed.

"I ordered pizza," he said as he came over and sat next to her, he switched the tv to a sports channel and stretched his legs out on the coffee table.

"I wanna take you and Kareem somewhere after we eat."

"Where?"

"It's a surprise," he gushed.

When Kareem had his fill, he staggered off to Trey who lifted him and took him outside on the patio. Kareem was fascinated with the world around him, he babbled at the birds and pulled at the foliage coming through the wooden bannister of the patio, many times, she had to stop him from eating the leaves hanging through.

Trey paid for the pizza and dropped the hot box on the counter, he plated slices for Jessica and himself and took two Fanta sodas from the refridgerator. Jessica ate one slice and fed small bites to Kareem, his drool was thick as he tasted the sweet flavor of the pepperoni, after she was finished she took him to his room and cleaned him off and changed his drool soaked top, she then sat at her vanity and prepped her face for the small trip, she kept a close eye on Kareem who was flinging her shorts from an open drawer.

Trey came up to get ready, he tossed his worn clothing in the laundry and headed into the shower, in the split second Jessica turned away to apply her mascara, she heard a loud shout, "Jessica," when she swiveled around and flew into the bathroom, Kareem was behind Trey screaming as the shower water soaked him from head to toe, "What are you doing in here?," she grabbed him quickly and stripped him out of the wet clothing and into dry comfy clothing, as soon as she tried to dry his hair, he started to fuss and search for her breasts, while he fed she gently patted his hair until it was dry. When he had fallen asleep, she placed him on the bed and finished getting ready.

Thirty minutes into the drive, Jessica had a pretty good idea where they were headed.

"These houses are gorgeous," she beamed. The houses were obviously owned or rented by wealthy individuals. She caught glimpses of the pools and manicured lawns behind the intricately designed gates.

"Yea, they are pretty dope."

It took Trey another thirty minutes before he arrived as his home on Carters. When they pulled up to the house, Jessica was not surprised. Just as he unsnapped Kareem from his seat, he woke in a screaming fit, he patted him on his back and apologised for disturbing him from his sleep and they all walked up to the front door.

"What's this little trip about?" she asked, stepping inside the door.

"I wanted to show you some changes I've made." Kareem began exploring his new home as soon as his feet touched the floor. Jessica followed him to the second bedroom, "This would be Kareem's room." The room was very big with a huge closet to match and it was move-in ready, it was also carpeted and the light blue curtains at the windows whipped around from the high breeze floating through the open windows. A chest filled with clothing stood against one wall with a small tv hung above it.

Trey kept a watchful eye over Kareem playing while Jessica inspected the room, there were boxes of pampers ranging up to sizes five and a few boxes of pull-ups, dress shirts and pants were hung in the closet with sandals and sneakers of varying sizes, the room looked better than the one he had at home with her.

"No, now isn't a good time," he whispered, he paused, listening to the person on the other end, "I'm a little busy, can I call you later?"

"Who was that?" her suspicion biting at her. She had no room to judge anyone but she was certain that he slept with his share of women, while he they were separated.

"A friend," he said, a little too fast.

She returned to the bedroom and Trey followed with Kareem in hand.

"This is really nice."

"Do you think he'd like it?" Kareem wriggled from Trey's arms and crawled directly to a pony that was standing next to the bed, as usual he licked it before realizing it wasn't edible.

"I have to show you the backyard."

He took Kareem up again and led her through the kitchen to the yard. The fenced yard was immaculate and the landscaped lawn was green and freshly mowed, the sparkling pool made her want to jump in, there was even an attached Jacuzzi and she figured he spent thousands on his little set up.

"So what I wanted to show you is right over here." He walked her to the northern side of the property to a newly built tree house. She stood at the bottom of the steps looking up at the wooden structure.

"Go up," he said.

She climbed the stairs slowly, catching at the tail of her dress as the high wind blew her dress into the air. "There's no one here but us, you can let it go." He felt the sudden growth in his pants and ignored it.

"How do you like it?" he asked, stepping inside, he set Kareem down and sat at the entrance of the tree house.

"I love it." They spent a few minutes in the tree

house while Kareem explored each box and toy he found, there were two windows on opposites sides of the house and you could actually stand up straight without touching the roof.

"I want my men to paint it. I already have the paint stored in the shed."

"It looks really nice, he's loving it as you can see."

"My uncle had one for his kids and we spent many days playing hide and seek or cops and robbers, I want him to have that same experience."

"That's super sweet."

They headed back down after twenty minutes, "Why didn't you tell me bring my swimsuit?" she asked, the pool looked delicious and she wanted to take a dip. No swimsuit, no problem, she thought, she unhooked her bra and pulled the straps through the arms of her dress, she then slipped out of her panties and tossed them in the deck chair and dived into the cool water. Trey turned when he heard the loud splash.

Jessica was swimming and making circles in the water, she swam up to the edge of the pool and took Kareem from Trey. Kareem was not crying this time, he slapped his hand in the water and smiled as it splashed in his eyes. The dress was now stuck to Jessica's skin and he could see her breasts clearly and the dark circles surrounding her nipples like saucers, he couldn't stop from thinking about having her hard pointy nipples in his mouth.

Jessica held Kareem by his arms allowing him to kick his legs in the water and she guided him up and down the pool slowly.

"I think it's about time he learns to swim," Trey said.

"There are a few clubs I've heard about, we can sign him up for one."

Jessica dunked her head beneath the water still holding Kareem up above the surface. They played for another twenty minutes before emerging from the pool. Jessica's dress stuck like glue to her body, she tried pulling it down as soon as her legs were out of the water but it was too late, Trey had already seen everything he needed too. She grabbed her bra and panties from the chair and headed inside. She rushed to the shower and washed her body off and then Kareem. Trey changed Kareem and Jessica tossed on one of Trey's t-shirts and boxer shorts while her dress dried in the dyer. She then sat with him on the couch.

"I have food and drinks, if you get hungry."

"I'm not hungry yet."

"So what do you think?"

"The pool is incredible; I *have* to take a dip in that Jacuzzi."

"Can you see yourself living here?"

She chuckled, "I'd be lying if I said no, the pool

alone would make me pack up and move."

"What's stopping you?"

Her eyes were glued to his, "I told you before I'm afraid and that's the honest truth."

He took her hand in his, "All we have to do is try." He saw the water settle in her eyes, "I'm serious, we can do this," he declared.

"What about Kareem? I already get up early as hell."

"I can manage him, all you would need to do is maybe feed him and dress him."

"It's gonna take me even longer to get home from work and the traffic, oh my gosh."

"So?" She pondered his invitation for a moment.

She took a deep shuddering breath. "Ok, we'll move in."

28

Back at home, Jessica looked around taking in her photos, furniture and her other worldly possessions, she sighed, she was excited but scared, she loved the sanctity of her home, she was felt safe there, soon she would be packing up and someone else would be enjoying her home.

"Penny for your thoughts?"

"What is our end game?" Kareem was asleep, so they had a while to talk. She walked into the living and sat on the couch. "Are we shacking up or we gonna get married again, what?"

"Of course, I want us to get married again, but the decision is ultimately yours, I don't want to force you into something you don't want to do."

"I'm fine with moving in with you, I just needed to know what the goal was behind you asking me to move."

"I want to raise our son as a family."

"I'm going to ask for time off to pack all of this up."

"Your boss is going to fire your ass with all this time off you keep asking for."

"Screw you. I make my quota."

She tucked her finger into his beard and pulled him to her, she kissed him slowly, teasing him with her tongue, he used his weight and planted her back into the couch, he stopped to kick his shorts off and then shifted the boxers she was wearing down her legs. He kissed her slit before coming back to her lips, "What was that?" she laughed, "Shhh," he said, he took her lips again as he powered into her, she yelped in pain, "I'm sorry baby," he stopped, concerned that he had hurt her, "I'm not even wet, shit that hurt," she said, she pushed his head down between her legs, he had to make it up to her...and that he did.

Jessica shook and trembled as electric bolts shot through her core in waves. She was still rolling from her climax when Trey rose above her and slammed into her again, her clit swelled and her walls creamed to Trey's enjoyment. "Fuck yes baby," "Aw shit," he belted out, five minutes later he expelled his load deep inside of her, the forceful release of his seed made him feel disoriented. He eased next to her breathing hard, half of his body rested on the couch and the other propped close to her breast, he was still inside of her and she could feel the warmness of his seed seeping into her, she stroked her clit slowly as she felt the strength of another sweet tingle, "Fuck, don't move," she begged, she arched her back and squeezed her legs tight against the sweet sensations exploding through her from her climax, Trey moaned as her spasms squeezed around his hard length and he instinctively rocked his hips into her, Jessica bucked and rubbed her clit rapidly, grunting and moaning as she came. Trey busted out laughing at her manic movements and as she came off of her high. She smacked his hand for laughing at her, it was so funny that she even began laughing.

"That's not funny," she said still cracking up.

"I wasn't really laughing at you," he said still laughing at her, "You are a freak my dear."

"So I've heard."

"From who?" his head shot up, he glowered at her waiting for a response.

Shit.

"My friends, you know I talk mad shit." She didn't feel like getting into a heated argument over her ex's, besides he knew she wasn't a virgin."

"Hmm, you need to be careful what comes out of your mouth," he said, kissing her hair.

Jessica tossed Trey from the couch and had him

remove the couch covers, she tossed them in the wash and went up to her bathroom to shower before Kareem woke from his nap.

Trey cleaned himself off while she took her shower and when she stepped out and grabbed her and rubbed his hard wood against her butt.

"Trey stoppp,"

"Just a quickie, I just want to feel you." He kept pulling her robe from out of her hands.

"No, we just had sex." Jessica needed to get her ass back on birth control, before he got her pregnant.

"Kareem is gonna be up soon, so no way."

Trey lifted her up under her butt and dropped her into the bed, he lightly nibbled her thighs and behind while she squirmed all over the bed, Jessica was laughing so much, she hardly could fight him, he licked her nipples before she could turn on her stomach trying to scramble off the bed, he held her two legs and dragged her back to him.

"Ow," she said as he bit her a little too hard on the back of her thigh.

"Sorry baby," he said still nibbling her body.

He flung her over and bit the tender flesh with between her legs.

"Trey stop," she pleaded softly. Her strength was waning fast.

Before she knew it, he was riding her steadily, they

shared needy, hungry kisses, as he filled her up entirely, enjoying each stroke and each throb of her slit as he reentered her stroke after stroke, "Trey I told you I didn't....want to have.....sex," she inhaled deeply through her nose as pleasure rumbled through her centre, "Don't talk, just enjoy it," he caressed her nipples, squeezing tiny droplets of milk from each breast, as he stroked her deeper and deeper, it took no less than two minutes before Jessica felt her body stiffen as a gush of her juices massaged the tip of his buried shaft. "He sucked her lips, the soft squishy sounds of their love making permeating the room, he raised her leg slightly and slipped into her two more inches, "Fuck Trey," she blurted, "Yes, baby, you feel sooo good," he said, just as he milked all of his cum inside of her. Jessica was sure she would be sore by morning.

Trey held his still pulsing shaft in his hand, small bubbles of cum settled on the top of its head and Jessica peered at the camera set up in her bedroom, Kareem was still sound asleep. He drew her close and she pulled away, annoyed.

"What's wrong?" he asked.

"Jess?"

"Negro, I didn't want to have sex, I didn't want to shower again, damn," she busted out laughing.

"Jess come on," he chuckled.

"And I'm gonna be sore as hell."

"Oh, I didn't know, you should have told me."

She looked at him and rolled her eyes.

"You can't say you didn't enjoy it!" he flashed her a huge grin.

She sucked her teeth and pushed off of the bed and washed off her body in the shower, she toweled off and walked back into the bedroom naked, Trey grabbed at her to pull her onto him and she shooed his hands away, she dressed into a short sundress and walked into Kareem's bedroom, from the camera on her side table she could see his tiny hands jerking back and forth.

"Kareem is up." She dashed off into his room and scooped him from his cradle. Kissing him she took him downstairs and fed him while she watched the tv.

29

"**G**ood Morning sweet boy," Trey pecked him lightly on his cheek. Kareem halted his feeding, looked at his father and returned to suckling.

"When do you want to start packing?"

"I guess we can start soon, there's not much I'm planning to take, just our clothing and my knit knacks, maybe you can order the boxes and start with my office stuff. I have a ton of photos and mementos in there."

"I have a few boxes I can start packing up the office." He got up and grabbed the boxes he had stored in his car for the move, he began packing her degree and photos into the box.

"What's this?" he handed her a crumpled cheque.

171

Shit. "It was a cheque from Ron...for Kareem." She could see from his face that he was upset.

"Why do you still have it?"

"I forgot I even had it." She had to tread lightly with Trey, fighting with him wasn't worth the aggravation.

"Mail it back to him, Kareem is not his responsibility."

"I tried giving it back, he didn't want it."

"Cool."

"Don't rip it," she screamed, "I'm thinking of donating it to Kareem's nursery or something." He ripped it anyway.

She folded her lips, swallowing the nasty retort bubbling behind her lips as Trey turned and went back to the office.

"Asshole," she said under her breath.

Kareem suddenly popped off of her breast and followed Trey into the office. She snickered triumphantly when she heard Trey repeatedly ask Kareem not to pull the items from the boxes he had already packed.

"Jessica!" he hollered. Jessica eased off the couch and tip toed out to the patio, closing the door softly behind her, she stretched her legs out on the bench listening to Trey fret and complain incessantly.

Jessica took her cell from the pocket of her dress and called her sister.

"Hey sissy, how are you?"

"I'm wonderful." Jessica said.

"What's up?"

"I'm just letting you know that we are moving to Treys."

"Ohhh, are we there yet?"

"I told him that I'd be willing to try, so yeah."

"Congratulations sissy."

"It's not congratulations, he asked me to try and I'm willing to try," she said dryly.

"You don't sound so enthusiastic, what are you feeling?"

"Nothing really, it's just that our track record is not the most appealing, I'm not certain if he'll ever trust me fully, our fights sometimes still end up back to Ron plus, picking up and moving is gonna be tough."

"Yeah but it's a new start. Don't you love him anymore?"

"I do...he's the one I've been waiting on, I'm happy right, but I'm scared to be happy cause I feel like some shit is gonna happen and then we are back at square one."

"I don't think that should be your main focus, Jess, if Trey didn't want you he wouldn't be asking you to move to Carters."

"You're right, I didn't look at it that way."

"It's a chance for new memories."

"For Kareem's sake I hope so."

"How's my nephew?" she asked, her voice brightening up.

"He's making Trey miserable." She laughed too damn hard for Trey.

"I know you heard me calling you?" He appeared at the door, highly annoyed.

"Char let me call you back." She stood and took Kareem from Trey, "Sorry I was on the phone."

He walked away pissed.

"Thanks sweetie," she called after him, smiling at Kareem, she said, "Daddy's mad at me baby." She put Kareem down and watched him pull at everything in sight while she chilled on the patio allowing him to explore until he started to eat the foliage.

Jessica laid on the floor while Kareem crawled over her, he struggled and took her breast from out of her dress, instead of feeding, he playfully yanked on her nipple, stretching it to the max with his gums and two teeth.

"No," she said sharply, "That hurts." He didn't like that his mother was spoiling his fun, so he set off to his dad.

Jessica took a look at her nipple and sighed. It was time for her to stop breastfeeding him before he bit her damn nipple off.

174

30

The celebration for Kareem's 1st birthday was in full swing and the house on Carters was filled with their family and friends. Jessica had even invited a few of the toddlers and their parents that she had befriended from the daycare. Jessica had moved into Trey's home, one month prior to Kareem turning one. Kareem thoroughly enjoyed discovering his new domain. It didn't seem like he noticed the changes in his environment. Their transition to the home at Carters went pretty smoothly since Jessica only packed clothing and her personal belongings, she planned to market her home as a fully furnished rental as soon as possible. If she had her way she probably wouldn't market it at all, in the event things didn't work out with Trey, she'd still have her home to go back to.

"He's gotten so big," Mrs. Clarke grinned, she held Kareem as he wiggled and pulled at the necklace around her neck.

"Yes he has," Alexus said to Olivia and Charmaine.

"I love the house," Rebecca said as she came up to the ladies.

"And the pool," Alexus drooled.

"It's impressive," Jessica agreed.

"How do you like it so far, being here with Trey?" Her mother asked.

"Actually, it's going pretty good, we have been connecting on an amazing level."

"I am genuinely happy for you hunny."

"Thank you mummy."

After the cake was cut, Jessica spent precious minutes trying to get Kareem to sit still for family photos, there were too many pretty balloons, kids and adults for him to stay in her arms for the photo taking session. After the photos were taken, Rebecca took Kareem into the pool and splashed around with him, he rubbed his eyes incessantly, wiping the water from his eyes, he was fascinated with the donut shaped inflatable pool toys and Rebecca held him upright while he inspected each one. When the pizza and ice cream were served, the children all dashed from the pool and devoured the delicious treats.

By the time the party ended two hours later, Trey had put Kareem down for his nap. He and Cameron cleaned up the deck and patio while the ladies cleaned the kitchen and mopped the floors before retiring to the freshly sanitized deck chairs.

"Where's Rebecca?" Alexus asked.

"She's changing," Jessica said.

"Hey, have you rented out your place as yet?" Olivia asked Jessica.

"Not as yet but I'd like to do it very soon though, I've just been too lazy to advertise my own shit."

"I'm thinking of moving closer to you guys, I'm going to put in my request for a transfer, once I get the approval, girl I'm moving in."

"That would be dope." Jessica said happily, "I wished we all lived closer to each other."

"Fuh real," Olivia agreed.

"How has Ron taken the...you know...change?" Alexus asked.

"I haven't spoken to him in a long time, he did message me once, wishing me all the best...asked me to take care of Kareem, yadda, yadda, yadda."

"That must have crushed him, having the son he thought was his, ripped from his arms like that, I wouldn't wish that on my worst enemy," continued Alexis.

"It would hurt anyone, I hope he finds the happiness he's looking for." Jessica joined in.

"Is he still with his wife?" Rebecca asked.

"I don't think so, she wasn't thrilled with the idea of him having a baby by me," she chucked the deuces real quick," Jessica said all too casually.

"Ron is a very nice looking man, I'm sure he has no problem keeping his bed warm at night," Olivia said and they all laughed out loud.

"Between him and Trey who is the better lover?" Olivia asked seductively.

Jessica nearly spit her drink out of her mouth, "A girl never kisses and tells," she said winking at Olivia.

"Oh come on, we're sisters," she wined.

"From what Charmaine said about the last time she came over your house unexpected, my pick would be on Ron." She worked her hips sensually as she spoke. Jessica shot Charmaine a nasty look and Charmaine looked away sipping her drink.

Everyone with the exception of Jessica hi-fived each other, snickering like silly school girls.

"Trey doesn't know any of that so quit it and change topics."

"All I'm saying is I'd love a man to ravage me now." Olivia continued to the delight of everyone, the scandalous conversation ended when Trey approached the ladies. "Rebecca your mother is ready to go," he said.

"Thanks Trey. Gotta go ladies, I wish I could stay and chat but duty calls."

"I guess we should all go. It's getting late."

"It's 7"00 p.m. Charmaine, pleaseeee." Olivia said annoyed.

"I'll walk you guys out." Jessica dipped into the kitchen and returned to the front door, she thanked her mother for coming and handed her a slice of cake for her father. After they had left she found Trey in the kitchen.

"When did Cameron leave?"

"Oh, when you guys were out on the deck."

"I'm gonna go crash, I have to be up early in morning.

"Cool." She kissed him lightly and took a quick shower before diving under the covers of the huge bed. The transition to living on Carters Boulevard was incredibly easy, even with the extra ten minute drive, she was still able to get to work on time plus with Trey dropping off and picking up Kareem, her load was ten times lighter. Moving was working out even better than she had imagined. Her relationship with Trey had also been an unexpected surprise, even though she thought she wasn't ready, she realized that she really did love him, their reuniting was one of the best relationship decisions she had made in a while, she was happy that she gave their relationship another chance.

Trey was over the moon that Jessica and his son were living together in his home, a home he'd bought just for them. Finally, she had gotten her ex out of her system and her focus was on him and Kareem. He had taken a giant gamble but he was thrilled that it had paid off, he was terrified that she would have fallen for Ron again, it would have killed him but he was now one hundred percent certain he could trust her again.

On this particular morning, Jessica drove directly to the first of several showings she had that day, as she sat outside of the first home waiting for her client to arrive, Jessica pulled out the home inventory list memorizing all the necessary specifications she needed to make her client aware of. While memorizing the list, her client pulled up and she exited her car.

They shook hands gracefully, "Hello Ramona, nice to see finally meet you."

"Hello Jessica, thank you for meeting me so early."

"My pleasure," Jessica said.

"You are stunning by the way."

"Thank you and so are you," she smiled.

"Thank you girl, the maintenance will kill you." Rebecca winked at her seductively.

Jessica didn't respond.

"Shall we?" She extended a hand to Ramona leading her to the front porch.

As they entered, they were greeted by a humongous foyer which opened up to a beautiful black wrought iron double staircase; the hanging chandelier in the centre of the high ceiling was equally as beautiful. They toured the four bedroom home for about an hour and Jessica fielded the numerous questions thrown at her. Ramona was a young rambunctious type, a little ditzy but cool.

"This is gorgeous." Ramona grinned.

"It is very unique design. The luxurious furnishings alone are well over five hundred thousand dollars."

As they toured the final rooms, Ramona blurted out "My boyfriend is eager for me to find us a place soon, he's very rich and very hot." The way she stressed on *hot* Jessica guessed he was very...hot.

"That's very..." she stopped herself, she was trying to stay professional.

"He wants to start a family right away, you know these successful older men," she said, tossing her very expensive virgin remy hair behind her back.

"His name is Ron Bishop, a super-rich investment banker. I'm sure you have heard of him."

"No, I'm sorry, I can't say that we've ever met."

Close to six hours later, she was on her way back to the office where she updated her database with her days' activities and then packed up for the day. Just as she was preparing to leave, her cell rang. She was anxiously awaiting this call. She listened intently to the caller for five minutes. After she ended the call, she crashed into her office chair, even though she had her suspicions, the news was still very much unexpected.

Jessica slung her purse over her shoulder and grabbed her work bag and headed to her car. She started her engine and turned the volume on her radio up and then lowered her driver's window, she loved the strong breeze against her face as it tousled her loosely styled hair. After forty-five minutes on the road, she pulled into the driveway and she grabbed her purse and bags and unlocked the front door, she dropped everything at the door and walked into the bedroom and stripped, she slipped into shorts and a t-shirt and went into the kitchen and started preparing dinner for her and Trey.

Jessica's mind was miles away from the meal she was preparing, she was nervous and scatter brained. She had something important to discuss with Trey and she wasn't sure how he would react or what the consequences would be. At 5:00 p.m., he and Kareem walked through the door.

"Hey baby." Trey said, he walked up to her and kissed her on the cheek.

"Hello handsome." She returned his kiss and she also kissed Kareem on his cheek.

Trey handed Kareem to Jessica while he went to the

room and changed, when he returned he sat on the living room floor with Kareem while he played with his toys. She checked on dinner and sat on the couch watching them play.

"I have something to tell you," she said cautiously.

"Shoot." He glanced between her and Kareem.

She paused before finding her voice, "I'm pregnant." The words stunned even her when they filtered into the room. Jessica had confirmed earlier with her doctor that she was indeed pregnant, she had to be certain before she broke the news to Trey.

"Fuh real?"

"Yes, I saw my doctor today and she confirmed it for me." She handed the small ultrasound image to Trey. She waited for a response from him.

He rushed to her and kissed her intensely, "I can't believe we're gonna have another baby," he kissed her again, "What made you think you were pregnant?"

"I was feeling sick again, like when I was pregnant with Kareem, so I made the appointment just to confirm my suspicions."

She saw the water appear in his eyes.

"How do you feel about being pregnant again?"

"I'm happy but I wasn't actually ready for another baby so soon," Trey stroked her stomach absent mindedly as she spoke, "But, I wasn't on any birth control, so there's that," she said softly.

"How far along do you think you are?"

"A few weeks."

"Can I tell my mother?"

"No baby, not yet, I'm not ready."

"I want to be at every appointment," he shouted in glee.

"Why is that?" she chuckled.

"When you were pregnant with Kareem, you know, we had the Ron issue, now with this new baby, we'd be starting from scratch for the most. I love Kareem, I love him with all of my heart, but I never really connected with you when you were pregnant, this is like a new chance for me," she wiped the tears from his eyes.

"I understand." She caressed his face softly.

He kissed her hand and held it in his.

"Why do I always have to wipe your tears away?" she smiled.

"'Cause you like wiping my tears away," he leaned in and kissed her again.

"Do you realize that we have to push the honeymoon back again?"

"Instead of a honeymoon, we can take a family trip."

"No sir, I want my honeymoon." She smiled.

His tone was stern and unwavering with his next words, "Jessica Sommers, will you marry again?"

She watched him closely before responding "Yes. I will."

While Trey rejoiced about his second marriage to the woman he loved and the birth of his second baby, there was a hard knock on the door, "While you get that I'll plate dinner," she said happily. Jessica returned to the kitchen pulling the plates from the cabinet.

From the kitchen she could hear whispers, Trey and whomever was at the door were whispering softly. Angry whispers. Jessica stopped moving, straining her ears to hear the conversation from her position in the kitchen. That was strange; he didn't invite the person in. Jessica stepped out of the kitchen, headed towards Trey. She couldn't see the visitor. Trey's body was blocking the person from sight.

"Trey, who's at the door?"

Trey jumped, startled by Jessica's voice behind him. He abruptly turned exposing the visitor. There at the door was a young woman, timid looking, petite and somewhat pretty, she was crying and when she saw Jessica she lowered her eyes and avoided making eye contact with her.

Jessica's eyes grazed over her slowly, taking in her big protruding belly. The white silk dress she wore stretched tightly across her huge baby bump. The stranger at the door was pregnant. Why the hell was she there? She'd never seen her before she thought.

Jessica's eyes travelled from the stranger at the door to Kareem sleeping over Trey's shoulder to Trey looking at her like he'd seen a ghost.

"Trey?" Jessica's voice was shaky and almost hoarse.

In that instant, Jessica realized two things; one, the universe was finally giving her a second chance and two; that second chance was coming with a big ass price, one she wasn't sure she was willing to pay.

THANK YOU

About The Author

Born and raised in the sunny Island of Barbados, this indie author is flexing her writing chops with her very first novel. A lover of romance and relationships, Debby-Ann has taken a unique approach to breathe life into the thoughts conceived in her fanciful mind's eye and when she is not thinking of a new tricky relationship to write about she is spending time with her family and friends.